About the Author

Chris Spring is an exhibiting artist and award-winning writer. His many published books and articles have been art historical in nature to date, celebrating the arts and cultures of Africa, with an emphasis on contemporary African art. They include *Angaza Afrika: African Art Now* (2008), *African Textiles Today* (2012), *African Art Close Up* (2013) and *South Africa, Art of a Nation* (2016) with John Giblin. Chris is a trustee of the October Gallery and an ambassador for the Africa Centre, London. TED & PTERRY is his first novel. Website: www.chrisspring.co.uk Instagram: @cjamesspring

Ted & Pterry

Chris Spring

Ted & Pterry

*Hope you enjoy
the book.*

All the best

Chris Spring

Olympia Publishers
London

www.olympiapublishers.com
OLYMPIA PAPERBACK EDITION

A CIP catalogue record for this title is
available from the British Library.

ISBN: 978-1-80074-298-7

First Published in 2022

Olympia Publishers
Tallis House
2 Tallis Street
London
EC4Y 0AB
Printed in Great Britain

Dedication

To all the Teds down the Samson and Delilah

Acknowledgements

Many thanks to Kristina Smith and the team at Olympia for making this such an enjoyable experience and to my old friend, Chris Winn for his great illustration on the cover of the book. Loving thanks also to my wife, Yvonne and to my children, Will and Maddie. Finally, I am eternally grateful to my dad, Mike and to my grandfather, the novelist, Howard Spring, both of whom encouraged me to write.

Chapter 1

Eddie's Blues

It's hard to believe that Paragon Road in Beckford, East London has ever lived up to its name, particularly on a grey Saturday in November when the pubs have shut for the afternoon and there's a thin drizzle in the air. In 1877 the mayor of Beckford might have felt justly proud when he first gazed upon Paragon Road's two neat terraces with their pretty front gardens. However, fast forward exactly a century and no whiff of paragon remains. A corrugated iron fence runs down one side of the road, and behind that there is a strip of waste ground where one of the terraces once stood. The other terrace is still standing, barely: the houses seem to be propped up against the grimy bulk of The Bloody Mary public house whose sturdy walls have also supported generations of the inhabitants of Paragon Road at chucking out time.

On a hot day earlier that year, Queen Elizabeth II had stopped briefly during her Silver Jubilee tour of East London to wave at the crowds gathered in front of The Bloody Mary, whereupon the landlady, Dolly Skeat—who had had one too many—fell down in a dead faint, as if her execution had been decreed. It had been the most exciting day in the history of Paragon Road.

At the other end of the road from The Bloody Mary stands Paragon Mansions. A glowering tower block erected in the late fifties as a monument to high technology and flash architects' fantasies of space-age urban living, it had reached out and devoured half the inhabitants of Paragon Road, pricking them out of their houses like winkles from their shells. In fact, Paragon Mansions is not really in Paragon Road at all, standing as it does in its own little 'estate'—a drab ring of grass covered with dog shit and broken bottles. But wherever you are in Paragon Road you can't get away from the Mansions. Even on the sunniest day there is a long black shadow right down the middle of the street.

No, there are not many paragons to be found in Paragon Road these days. One of the elderly high-rise inhabitants, pausing for a moment and gazing down from the twentieth floor of the Mansions at the remains of the street, might even have felt glad that he had been re-housed. But if, instead of returning to his TV on this particular day, he had bothered to look out of his window a little longer, he would have noticed something quite remarkable happening in Paragon Road after all.

A paragon of sorts did appear, a paragon with a deep lustre to its perfect red and cream body, a paragon with white-walled tyres and plenty of chrome, cruising—almost strutting—down the road like a peacock in a chicken run, before drawing serenely into the kerb and coming to a halt as far as possible from the other shabby cars. It was a fifty-nine Vauxhall Velox, and on that dull November afternoon it arrived on Paragon Road like the sun coming out.

The driver of the car didn't immediately get out. Perhaps he wanted to give the inhabitants of Paragon Road a few moments to catch their breath, for when he did emerge from the leopard-skin lined interior, it became apparent that he was only slightly less extraordinary than his car. True, his bodywork was in some need of repair, as it was suffering from the ravages of beer and chips, but the rest of him was magnificent. He wore a powder-blue, finger-tip length drape jacket with black velvet collar and Vandyke cuffs. Beneath that, a white shirt and gold lamé waistcoat was stretched tautly over his paunch. Black drainpipe trousers shot from the confines of the lamé and ended well above his ankles, which were encased in blue Day-Glo socks. A bootlace tie, two-tone winklepickers, curling at the points, and thick-rimmed dark glasses completed the picture. In short, he was a Teddy Boy and one of the finest examples of his kind.

He was thirty-seven years old and his name was Edward Caldecott, Eddie to his acquaintances. If anyone called him Ted, he looked the other way. In view of his chosen lifestyle, he thought it undignified in the same way as it would be if you called a vicar 'Vic' just because he was unfortunate enough to have been christened Victor. Eddie's parents always called him Ted, but Eddie was usually looking the other way when they spoke to him anyway, so it didn't matter so much.

Eddie leaned back against the beautiful, rounded wing of the Velox, crossed one drainpipe over the other, and began to roll a cigarette, expertly, using only his left hand. With his right hand he felt in the pocket of his drape jacket, pulled out a Zippo petrol lighter, flipped open the lid and lit up. He held the cigarette between thumb and forefinger, with the rest of his hand cupped protectively around it, the glowing point almost touching his palm. The distinctive opening chords of

Eddie Cochran's *Three Steps to Heaven* drifted through the open window of the Velox. Eddie Caldecott shifted his feet.

Something about the sound had changed the set of his face. He took a long drag on his cigarette, because behind his dark glasses tears had begun to form. He would never admit it, but one of the reasons he wore the shades was to hide the tears that crept into his eyes when he was moved by something. He had caught this happening more and more often recently—it wasn't just when he felt moved by Eddie Cochran songs (which he regarded as permissible), but also by the people in his life, and events which previously wouldn't have affected him at all. It worried him to feel such strong emotions, and it especially bothered him when they caused the drops on his eyelashes to unite and trickle out down his cheeks from behind his dark glasses. Eddie reached into the Velox, turned off the music, wound up the window and locked the door. Then he threw down the butt of his cigarette and screwed it into the tarmac with one decisive movement of his Cuban heel.

*

A few hundred yards away, an old man paused on a bridge and looked out across the broad stretch of water formed by the confluence of the Hackney Cut and the Hertford Union canal. He didn't normally stop there because he was usually hurrying on his way between the Bombay Grab public house and the betting shop on Bladebone Lane, but this afternoon something had caught his attention and pulled him up short. The drizzle had stopped, and though it was still very gloomy, a gap had opened between the clouds and the land. It was filled with a dirty reddish light that threw the warehouses, gas holders and factory chimneys which made up the skyline into sharp silhouette. A thin, slanting finger of light fell to earth somewhere beyond the Isle of Dogs, while another fell between Rotherhithe and Limehouse. A jetliner passed through the first beam of light, flashing bright gold for a moment against the grey of the sky.

It was this scene which caught and held the imagination of the old man on the bridge. It reminded him of similar scenes he had witnessed from this bridge when he was younger, only then the reddish light on the skyline hadn't been made by the sinking sun but by a thousand fires in the docks: the fingers of light had reached up from the ground instead of falling from the sky, and the air had been full of the sounds of bells and sirens, the throb of aircraft engines, the crump of bombs and above all the fiendish roar of fire, in contrast to the silence which pervaded the present scene. It was a silence peculiar to those areas of the city which once had been full of sounds and no longer are—a silence you never hear in the country.

As the old man continued to gaze from the bridge, he began to remember other things from those days, apart from the hardship and suffering. He remembered the comradeship and the laughter, the new friends he made and the blackouts—most of all he remembered the blackouts and Ethel, soft under the dining room table or in the Anderson Shelter. They had made love as if the world would end tomorrow, as it had done for so many people at that time. As the old man's memories flowed, the tears began to form in his eyes before trickling down his cheeks and dropping into the creeping waters of the canal.

At that very moment, the fruit of one of those passionate blackouts with Ethel appeared on the towpath directly below him—a winkle-pickered war baby by the name of Edward Caldecott.

'Oh blimey,' he said as he caught sight of his son. 'What are you bleeding doing down there, Ted, eh, eh? If you're late for tea again, your mother'll go spare.'

Eddie raised an arm in acknowledgement but didn't stop or look up—he was a man of few words. The old man watched his son for a few moments, then spat in the canal and walked on down towards the Bombay Grab. The clouds had thickened again, putting out the searchlights and fires down at the docks of his memories.

Eddie continued along the towpath and turned up the Hertford Union until he was out of sight of his dad. Then he stopped, took a piece of brown paper out of his pocket, unfolded it, placed it carefully on a bollard and sat down. Eddie liked being by the canal on dull Saturday afternoons— it made him feel relaxed and in control, preparing him for the evening to come. He rolled a cigarette with great care, put it in his mouth and leaned forward, rubbing his hands together and looking up and down the canal. Normally he would have allowed himself a smile at this point, but not this afternoon. He had things on his mind – weighty things, like the tears, which he could not come to grips with. He reached thoughtfully for the Zippo and lit up, letting the smoke find its way out of his mouth for a few seconds before blowing the rest across the canal. At that moment, a cloud of steam oozed from the brick wall opposite, the breath of some hidden monster, while further off a tall chimney wearing a funny hat blew three regular blasts of black exhaust into the darkening sky.

'Shippam's!' exclaimed Eddie. He had promised to stop swearing so much, and his girlfriend Maureen had told him to think of something really horrible when the urge to swear came upon him. Such a thing of horror for Eddie was Shippam's Bloater Paste.

Eddie sent his fag end flying out into the canal and started off up the towpath again. The blasts had reminded him that he had promised to give up smoking as well as swearing, but worse still—he had remembered that yet another rockabilly group, with its attendant skins and punks, would be playing at The Samson & Delilah that evening.

Rockabilly was a curious, furious hybrid consisting of boogie-woogie, rhythm and blues, swing and southern hillbilly music which had had its heyday in the US during the mid-to-late fifties, but then re-emerged in the mid-seventies in England with an almost fanatical cult following, as an offshoot of the wider rock 'n roll revival. For Eddie, as for many of the other Teds, rockabilly was definitely not rock 'n roll as he understood it, and if there was one thing in life he couldn't stick it was a skin/rockabilly kid. Smooves, Oi!s and Greasers, Rude Boys and Rastas—they were all a joke. He would have the occasional dust-up with them, but basically, they didn't impinge on Eddie's world. In fact, he liked to know they were there, poor fools, missing out on the best things in life. But rockabilly skins—you couldn't get away from 'em. They were there at every rock 'n roll pub and party in their dirty jeans, Doc Martens and donkey jackets, raving about some crazy, redneck farmer with a twangy guitar who cut twenty discs in a cowshed somewhere outside Chattanooga in 1957, and trying to tell everyone in the gaff that this was pure WHITE MUSIC, whites only rock 'n roll.

Eddie was no liberal, but he could smell shit when it was being dealt, and he knew enough about the history of rock 'n roll to know that rockabilly had its roots as much in 'black' music as in 'white,' if not more so—the fact that it had mainly been performed by white bands was just another case of the whites pinching what wasn't really theirs in the first place.

'All check shirts and chicken shit,' muttered Eddie as he walked along, allowing himself a little smile at his well-used witticism.

'No one to blame but ourselves,' he went on, the smile disappearing from his face.

He and the other 'originals' had seen it coming for years. It had started with a handful of DJs in the 'rock historian' mould plugging the sound over the airwaves, then some smart record company executives bought the masters of the songs for next to nothing and put them on compilation albums. Then came the rush of home-grown bands catering for the growing demand, and finally a plague of fans, mostly young kids who dug the frantic rhythm like a drug to the point where they weren't prepared to listen to anything else. They wanted to be different, but they weren't prepared to accept and understand the romance of rock 'n roll in its true sense, or the sartorial, social and musical demands of being a real Teddy Boy—so Eddie thought, at least, though he might not have put it quite in those words. He was a man of few words.

*

The sky darkened. A thin mist slunk like fag smoke across the still surface of the canal. Beneath the low brick bridges, it looked almost like night, especially to a man wearing sunglasses. Emerging from the shadow of one of the bridges, Eddie stopped short and stared into the depths of the canal where he saw himself reflected between the decaying skeleton of an old pram and the still gleaming cage of a supermarket trolley. In that reflection one of his worst fears had been realised, the inescapable truth he finally had to face up to—he was almost bald.

Neither the splendour of his sideburns nor the monumental quality of the DA (duck's arse) on the back of his neck could any longer compensate for the sad ripple which had once been a mighty bow wave on his forehead. His knees felt weak at the sight. He had always known deep down that the facts about his forehead would have to be faced, but he hadn't bargained for their crushing impact on his self-esteem. His hand shook as he felt in the breast pocket of his drape and produced a small metal comb with which he attempted to manoeuvre the ripple into something like its former glory, but this served only to jerk a few more precious hairs from their greasy follicles.

At that moment, the sound of suppressed laughter from the bridge above made him look up. As he did, he missed seeing a dark, sinuous shape that slid between the surface of the canal and the submerged pram and trolley. A Standard 'Little Demon' came fizzing over the parapet and went off with a loud bang at Eddie's feet, momentarily lighting him up and enveloping him in smoke like some comic villain in a melodrama. The sound drowned out the splash made by the dark shape which had reared up behind Eddie, but which now fell back into the water.

'I'll kill yer,' shouted Eddie, looking up and hurling the nearest projectile to hand—his small metal comb sailed clean over the bridge and landed with a plop on the other side, where it was swallowed by the dark shape before it reached the bottom of the canal. He didn't see the children but heard the sound of running feet and laughter dying away into the distant mutter of traffic. 'Bloaters' he shouted, then chuckled quietly to himself. A few hundred yards ahead of him, the same dark shape reared up from the depths of the canal and disdainfully spat Eddie's comb onto the towpath.

*

Eddie loved kids. His girlfriend Maureen had two, Ronnie and Derek. They were twins, but you wouldn't have known they were even brothers, so different were they to look at. Ronnie was plump and docile, and tall for his ten years. Derek was small, stray-cat thin and twice as streetwise, with skin and hair that were darker than Ronnie's – his habit of looking to the left and right with a twitch of his head and a sniff of his nose gave him the appearance of being keyed up and alert at all times. Eddie would probably have had some kids of his own if his marriage had lasted more than a few months, but that had been almost twenty years ago. Maureen hadn't had much choice with Ronnie and Derek—she could hardly remember their father, though sometimes she had the vague feeling that he had been more like Derek than Ronnie. Anyway, they had been as good as sons to Eddie for the last ten years.

Eddie remembered his dad's words a few weeks before,

when he had caught him playing on the swings in Springfield Park with Ron and Derek: 'Come on, Ted, admit it, you're no more than a great big overgrown schoolboy. Look at yerself if you don't believe me.' Well, he might be right, and maybe that was why Eddie hadn't been angry at the kids who threw the Little Demon at him—after all, they could just as easily have been Ron and Derek.

Eddie knew they'd be at Upton Park this afternoon with Maureen. Eddie didn't much like football and Maureen adored it, so she usually took Ron and Derek when the Hammers were at home, despite the racism which they often had to endure, even in the family enclosures. The brilliant Clyde Best, one of the few black players in the First Division, had just ended a distinguished playing career for the Hammers, which had made them proud—and their lives a little easier. The twins always pleaded with Eddie to come, but there were too many skinheads at the games again nowadays, and Eddie didn't want any aggravation, though he never let on that this was one of the reasons why he didn't go.

The Little Demon had done a lot to blow away Eddie's blues, at least for the time being. Besides, it was now so dark that Eddie couldn't clearly see his reflection in the canal, and the awful truth about his hairline had once more receded. He also consoled himself with the thought that at least he would never stoop so low as Willie the Wig, one of the Teds at The Samson and Delilah who, to hide his baldness, had had a special toupee made with a bow wave attachment. Far from solving Willie's problems, it had made him the laughing stock of the pub.

No, in the gathering, comforting darkness, even the

prospect of an evening with the rockabillies didn't bother him so much, and he put the tears which had been catching him out in recent months firmly to the back of his mind.

Eddie began to walk again, following the canal, which crept through a canyon of brick for the last few hundred yards of its course to the Limehouse basin. But almost immediately he stopped and looked down. There on the towpath, glimmering in the fading light, was his metal comb.

'Shhhhippam's,' he whispered, 'can't be.' As he bent to pick it up his nostrils filled with an alien stink: he was standing beneath an effluent pipe out of which some prehistoric fluid was continually dripping, causing strange tropical grasses to spring up in towering abundance on the towpath beneath, their jointed stalks now leafless and white with the onset of winter. After a momentary pause, he thought better of picking up the comb.

'Must be somebody else's,' he whispered beneath his breath and quickened his pace as he approached the lock-keeper's cottage. Although he had heard it a thousand times before, he flinched involuntarily at the ferocious barking of the two Alsatians chained outside. In the gloomy light it seemed as though he was being menaced by a single creature from whose body issued at least three fearsome heads set with shining eyes and white, gnashing teeth. A curtain was pushed aside, a hand rubbed away the condensation from the window and a face peered out into the night – but by then Eddie was out of sight. He paused and listened as the dogs' barking seemed to turn into yelps of terror and pain for a moment before silence once more descended.

A great wooden gate blocked the towpath at the mouth of the tunnel that led to the Limehouse basin. Eddie leaned against the gate and drew several deep breaths. He hated feeling ruffled, having spent almost all his adult life trying to project a state of permanent 'cool'. But deep down, he had to admit that there were few kicks to compare with passing the dogs and coming unseen to the mouth of the tunnel. He knew that the lock-keeper probably didn't give a monkey's who went through to the basin, but that only increased the enjoyment for Eddie—after all, he didn't really want to upset anybody by trespassing or breaking the law, he just wanted the satisfaction of doing it for its own sake.

The mighty gate gave a satisfyingly gothic groan as Eddie swung it aside. He looked around furtively to make sure no one was watching, then disappeared into the tunnel.

Chapter 2

Twenty Flight Rock

In 1942, the Limehouse basin had resembled a sprawling kitchen full of cursing, sweating, lighter men struggling to feed the mouth of the Grand Union canal and the Lea Navigation. (Lighters were the flat-bottomed barges specially designed for use on canals, which required very particular skills of the men who used them.) Throughout the day and into the night, the great gates of the lock would open, either to admit narrow boats with their laden lighters or 'butties' in tow, beginning the long haul north, or to disgorge empty lighters returning from Birmingham or Manchester where their cargoes had been swallowed up in the almighty effort to keep the country armed and fed. Now, thirty-five years later, there was hardly a ripple in the slick black surface of the water in the basin, not a movement on the bare, deserted quays and wharves, only Eddie emerging from the tunnel, looking rather self-conscious, and adjusting his shades and bootlace tie. Nobody noticed him, which wasn't surprising as there were only six other people in the vast area of the basin.

Eddie gazed with satisfaction at the desolate, mournful scene spread before him. The lack of activity suited his mood just fine. For over thirty years he had been coming to the Limehouse basin, and year by year he had seen the water traffic dwindling, and the towpath becoming less busy. Now, it was unusual for him to see more than a handful of other people on the whole length of the walk. As the years passed, he had come to think of this little world and its mysterious landscape as a secret to which he alone was a party: a reservoir of memories, of sights, smells and sounds which he could draw on when he returned to the outside world. He got ready to sit down on his favourite bollard and felt in his pockets for the brown paper. 'Shippam's Paste!' he muttered, remembering he had left it behind when he had sat down at the entrance to the Hertford Union. It wasn't like Eddie to forget things like that, even if his mind had been troubled at the time. He sat down anyway.

Along the wharf to his left, a fisherman sat beside a glowing brazier, with one side of his face lit up, the other in shadow. He was leaning forward with his elbows resting on his knees in an attitude of prayer as he peered down into the water. Three other points of light around the basin showed that other anglers were engaged in their seemingly thankless vigil. Eddie had never seen them catch anything but door mats and dead dogs. A few years earlier, he had had the temerity to ask one of them '''Ad any luck, mate?' The man made no reply, so Eddie went on, 'What're you after, then?'

'Eels, mate—and it's not luck, it's skill,' replied the angler without turning around or even moving from his position.

At that point, Eddie had realized in his heart that he had broken one of the cardinal rules of the canal—humans in the landscape are not to be seen as animate objects and should no more be communicated with than bollards or spiked railings.

From where he sat, Eddie couldn't see the other two

people who were sharing the basin with him and the anglers. One of them was listening to the football results in a neon-lit hut by the main gates, while the other stood in the doorway of a derelict building on the far side of the basin, close to the lock which led out under Narrow Street into the Thames. From time to time she moved out of the shadow into the light cast by the street lamps in Narrow Street. Then you could see that she was quite young and dressed up to the nines.

Eddie deftly rolled a cigarette. Above him the clouds had opened to reveal a ragged patch of sky, tinted the most delicate shade of yellowy green, and studded with a few faint stars. It had already seemed like night for so long that this last glimpse of daylight came almost as a miracle to the Limehouse Basin. The hole in the clouds widened and the reflection of the sky spread rapidly across the surface of the water like a drop of petrol on a drab puddle. Eddie lit his fag, took a drag and leaned forward, rubbing his hands together, partly to keep them warm but mostly as a gesture of satisfaction at the feast set before him. As the clouds cleared, the familiar landmarks on the horizon began to appear. In the distance, he saw cooling towers and a gas holder, almost indistinguishable in the haze. Slightly closer, there was a church spire and two factory chimneys, one fat, one thin. Just across the basin was a group of cranes that hadn't moved for months, hooks hanging forlornly as if angling for a cargo which would never come again. Closer still, the great prows of several dredgers, with their chains of rusty scoops running down into the water, were looking more than ever like the bony-plated necks of prehistoric creatures stooping to drink.

Eddie looked to the left and right, rubbed his hands together again and allowed himself half a smile. He flicked his fag end out into the basin, watched it fall, watched it fizzle out as it hit the water, then saw the tiny concentric ripples spreading out across the surface—that's how still it was. The wind that had taken the clouds out of the sky hadn't yet come down to earth. Eddie shifted his gaze slightly to the reflection of a jetliner which had begun to crawl, insect-like, across the surface of the water beneath his bollard. As he followed the soundless course of the plane, the smile disappeared from his face, and was replaced by a frown. In five months' time, on April 17th, he would be thirty-eight years old, and Eddie Cochran would have been dead for exactly eighteen years.

*

Eddie vividly remembered the day Cochran had died and how he had heard the news of his death. He had been at a fair on the Hackney Marshes for most of the day, celebrating his birthday with Sylvia Gibbs. Sylvia lived in Swinburne Road, Leytonstone, which was definitely a social notch or two above Paragon Road. They were due to be married that June, despite opposition from Sylvia's parents, who thought that she was marrying beneath her. Sometimes Sylvia thought her parents might be right, but the creepy short-back-and-siders which they offered as alternatives to Eddie only convinced her that she was making the right decision. Eddie had driven to Bristol with her the day before, to see the last concert of Cochran's British tour.

'I'll be back,' shouted Cochran at the end of the show, and thousands of Teds roared their approval, including Eddie, resplendent in his brand-new, off-the-peg Burton drape. He had looked so handsome driving back at the wheel of the Zodiac: at that moment, Sylvia was convinced that she was making the right choice.

Late in the afternoon of the following day, they were strolling arm in arm towards the Ferris wheel for one last ride before going back to the Zodiac for a bit of passion. Eddie bought an Evening News before they got onto the big wheel—he liked to sit reading while Sylvia sat screaming. The car rose into the air and Sylvia closed her eyes and began to scream. When they reached the highest point from the ground, Eddie stood up and set the car rocking with an expert sway of his body, then sat down and opened his paper. He saw the story almost at once, read a few lines, then let the paper drop to the floor of the car. He closed his eyes and saw the accident, the Ford Consul leaving the wet road, the wreckage against a lamppost, the ambulance and Cochran's quiet ending in hospital a few hours later. In the distance, he heard Sylvia screaming—when she opened her eyes and saw the expression on Eddie's face, she screamed some more and went on screaming through ten revolutions of the wheel. Eddie sat motionless through all this, with his eyes closed, and as the wheel revolved an idea began to form in his mind.

It was small and wispy to start with, like the first windings of candy floss on a stick, then rapidly growing into a woolly, bright pink puff, so that by the time he stepped from the car at the end of the ride, he had convinced himself that he was the reincarnation of his hero. It all fitted. His birthday on the day of Cochran's death, the same Christian name, the same initials E.C. Cochran's last words 'I'll be back' now seemed prophetic. Sylvia had been violently sick down the side of the car. 'I wanna go home, Eddie,' she sobbed, wiping an undigested winkle from the corner of her mouth and trying in vain to resculpt her peroxide coiffure.

Eddie drove her home to Leytonstone, then returned to 91 Paragon Road via the off-licence, where he bought a bottle of Bell's and a quart of Whitbread Pale. Eddie's father had seen the Zodiac pull up and went to open the door. 'Oh bli...' Eddie pushed past him before his father's habitual greeting had been fully delivered, and by the time Ethel Caldecott came out into the hall with the birthday cake she had just baked, Eddie was already locked in his room with the first of many choruses of 'Summertime Blues' pumping out of the Dansette, and the first whisky beginning the work which was to keep the bathroom occupied and reverberating for most of the night while Albert, in his vest and trousers, and Ethel, in her dressing gown and slippers, sat on the stairs outside.

Throughout the summer of 1960, Cochran's *Three Steps to Heaven* was in the British charts, and Eddie spent those months developing his own personal mythology. He was slimmer then, and had a good mop of black, greasy hair so that, with some expert sculpting and if the light was in the right direction, he could present a passable resemblance to his dead hero and alter ego.

Eddie married Sylvia in June as he had promised, and they moved into a flat on the twentieth floor of the newly built Paragon Mansions. They could have had a flat on the first floor, but Eddie had specifically asked for the twentieth, mainly because he'd be nearer to heaven (and to Cochran) and because he would also be able to act out Cochran's song *Twenty Flight Rock*:

'But she lives on the twentieth floor uptown...

The elevator's broken down.'

As it happened, the lift in the Mansions didn't break down immediately, and for a while the novelty of the view from the flat, especially on long summer evenings, did make Sylvia feel, if not actually nearer to heaven, at least different. It seemed a privilege to be up so high, away from the heat and dust of the streets below, and she even found it in her heart to forgive Eddie for making her feel he had taken the vows with Eddie Cochran rather than with Sylvia Gibbs.

Then winter came and the white walls of the Mansions became streaked with grey: impurities oozing from the concrete and the accumulation of city grime blown up from the streets or falling in the rain. Sylvia began to hear complaints from other occupants who got onto the lift at lower floors: 'half a ton fell on my bed while I was sleepin'... 'bleedin' thing come right off in my hand'... 'wasn't half a funny colour'... 'smelled something dreadful it did...' But she tried to turn a deaf ear and literally turned her back on them—she had already established a slight air of superiority over people from the flats below.

Then one morning two long cracks appeared in the bedroom wall, and shortly afterwards a patch of fungus began to spread across the ceiling of the tiny, windowless bathroom. For two months Sylvia begged Eddie to do something, then she moved on to threatening him until he finally took action. Eventually, the council workers responded to his requests, and tried and failed to repair the damage. 'The whole building's rotten,' they volunteered, by way of explanation. The council offered the Caldecott's another flat about a mile away, on the third floor, but Eddie had set his heart on their present accommodation, and he wasn't going to budge.

'Eddie!' Sylvia said in a shrill voice from behind a wagging finger one morning: 'I'm not asking you again, if you haven't done anything about this place by the time I get back from work, I'm... I'm leaving you.' She choked back a tear, visibly moved by the melodramatic statement she had just made, but then took a grip on herself, drew a deep breath and stormed out of the flat, slamming the door behind her. The authoritative clip-clipping sound of her stiletto heels faded into the other sounds of the city.

Eddie was out of work and had time on his hands, but unemployment breeds apathy, and it wasn't until late afternoon that he stirred himself to do something about Sylvia's threat. He moved a wardrobe so that only the tops of the cracks were visible and painted the bathroom ceiling with white emulsion. Then he put on his best drape and went down to The Samson and Delilah where he now enjoyed what amounted to a cult following among the local Teds. Sylvia normally came to join him later. She had stayed at home to cook his dinner on a couple of occasions during the first few weeks of their marriage, but Eddie had never been in much of a state to appreciate her cooking after an evening in the Samson, so now she was resigned to a chip shop dinner after their visits to the pub—which seemed to happen most evenings.

But that night she didn't come. Eddie drank more than his normal six pints and indulged in a good deal of maudlin sentimentality over Eddie Cochran, followed by short bursts of violent abuse directed at any luckless Ted who didn't seem to be paying sufficient attention. In the Zodiac on the way back to the Mansions, he was drunk enough to briefly contemplate acting out the ultimate parallel between himself and his idol—any lamppost would have done the job. However, there was still something deep inside him, telling him he wasn't Cochran and never would be, and that as sure as the sky was blue, he would survive to be fat and forty.

This notion sent him into a gloom that lasted almost to the turning into Paragon Road, but then he started to think of Sylvia, dressed in a Baby Doll nightie, standing in front of the stove preparing his dinner. He shifted in his seat as the image began to excite him. 'That's why she didn't come down to the Samson,' he thought, 'she's seen what I did, and she's cooking me a surprise dinner to say thank you...'

When Eddie reached the Mansions there was an 'out of order' notice on the lift gate. Eddie smiled with satisfaction and shambled round to the stairs, yodelling as he went:

'We-e-ell I've got a girl with a record machine,

When it comes to dancin', she's the queen

All alone on a Saturday night

I love to hold and-a-squeeze her tight

But she lives on the twentieth floor uptown

Elevator's broken down.'

Eddie began to climb...

'So, I walked one, two flight, three flight, four—

Five, six, seven flight, eight flight more...'

Eddie's breath was coming in short gasps now, interspersed with enormous inhalations...

'Got to the twelfth I'm a-startin' to drag...'

Lights were flashing before his eyes...

'Sixteenth-a-floor I's startin' to sag...'

He pulled off his bootlace tie and spat down the stair well, his stomach heaving, heart thumping...

'Got to the top—I's too tired to rock!'

But there was no one to rock with, even if he had been capable of it—the flat was empty. Eddie just made it to the windowless bathroom before his protesting stomach finally ejected its contents, and as he tilted back his head from the toilet bowl, he saw the brown ring of fungus standing out boldly on the ceiling through his new paintwork, making him fear the worst. Sure enough, when Eddie finally staggered into the bedroom, he found a handwritten note pinned to the pillow. Sylvia had gone to Leytonstone, and she would not be coming back.

Chapter 3

Something Else

Eddie sat on his bollard by the Limehouse basin grinning guiltily at the memories and looking for all the world like an outsize garden gnome perched on a toadstool. No one could possibly mistake him for Eddie Cochran now. He looked up at the sky to search for the jetliner whose reflection he had been following and, as he did so, a long, dark shape like a sinuous submarine passed just below him. By the time Eddie's gaze returned to the water, its surface was undulating slightly, but it soon became glassy calm again. Then there was the image of the jetliner, almost directly below him now, still moving slowly and soundlessly across the surface. He was so absorbed in thought, he didn't notice that one of the 'dredgers' had disappeared, or that a few moments later, the point of light from an angler's brazier on the far side of the basin suddenly went out.

*

Sylvia was as good as her word—she never came back to the Mansions. Eddie cried a bit, raged a bit and felt extremely sorry for himself. For a while he made the most of his loss, threatening to do all sorts of romantic things like drive the

Zodiac off Beachy Head, but none of it ran very deep. In the end, he came to respect Sylvia for having had the courage to call it off instead of having let the marriage meander on as he would have done.

Eddie stayed on in the Mansions thanks to an oversight by the council. He licked his wounds, restored his pride, and worked at his image. He got a job as a postman but found it hard to read the addresses on the letters. One day the doctor told him he needed glasses, which put Eddie in a panic for a while, as he knew Cochran had never worn them. When he got back to the flat, he looked through his photos of Cochran and discovered a few where the man was wearing sunglasses. So, he went down to the opticians in Stallion Street the next day and blew almost a week's wages ordering a pair of prescription sunglasses. He was nervous about the Teds' reaction down at the Samson, so he waited until his birthday, the second anniversary of Cochran's death, which he judged to be a suitable day to make an appearance wearing the shades. Meanwhile the ratepayers of Beckford had to spend their time sorting out and redelivering each other's mail.

'Mark of respect,' he was going to say if anyone questioned him about the shades, but he needn't have worried—his influence was such that he could have come in wearing a white sports coat and a pink carnation and the Teds would still have thought it cool.

It was April 1962, and the heyday of rock 'n roll was long gone—Holly, Cochran, Richie Valens and the Big Bopper were dead, Presley had sold out to the movies and the charts were full of crooners, balladeers and teen starlets called 'Bobby' chirruping anodyne love chants. Within a year, it would all be swept away. When the Mersey Sound arrived, many of the Teds combed out their bow waves and washed the Tru-Gel from their hair, or simply got married and 'grew up.' Not Eddie. He had a reputation to maintain, and in his eyes, it would have been blasphemous even to contemplate change. So, there was a missionary zeal in his approach to preserving his lifestyle and that of the other Teds who chose to stick with him. All around the country, similar groups of fanatical 'originals' were forming. There were an increased number of fights at the Samson, and it changed management. When it re-opened, Teds were temporarily banned from the premises, so for a while Eddie took to travelling up to The Jackdaw in Edmonton or down to The Green Man in Bow until The Samson and Delilah opened its doors once more to the Teds.

As his belly spread and his hair receded, Eddie gradually phased out his Cochran reincarnation theory and adopted instead a particular brand of moroseness which filled his fellow Teds with a certain sheepish sense of awe. He had few real friends at the time and that suited him fine. He was content to watch through the bottom of a beer mug as the brightly coloured, sickly smelling, jangling cavalcade of the sixties passed by.

*

Early in 1970, Eddie got himself a job as a gravedigger. He treated this as the ultimate cool, as it set him apart from all the chippies, clippies, sparks and brickies down at the Samson. One bright spring morning, a couple of years later, when he was up to his eyeballs in his thirty-second grave, he looked up from his work to find himself being observed by two tiny persons, leaning over the safety bar of their pram, their round puckered faces wearing that expression of open-mouthed, slack-jawed bewilderment which only babies can produce. Behind them, he saw Maureen's larger, longer, but equally expressive face wearing its cap of tightly curled black hair. She was working hard to suppress her laughter. In response, Eddie opened his mouth and guffawed—it was an unusual but strangely pleasant sensation for him. Maureen finally laughed too, relieved by his reaction. The twins continued to look puzzled, not sure whether to laugh or burst into tears.

Maureen came to the graveyard every morning that week. They talked about their lives and this and that, with the twins always present as interested but uncomprehending spectators. At the end of the week, Eddie accepted Maureen's invitation to supper to celebrate his birthday '... and taste some real Caribbean cooking—Lord knows what you've been feedin' yourself all this time!'

It was love at first sight—whenever they thought about each other, it was always that initial picture in the graveyard which came to mind first. For his part, Eddie had fallen in love with all three of them: to begin with, he could barely conceive of them as separate people. The twins joined by the pram to Maureen often seemed to form an individual creature in its own right. Even when the twins began to grow and develop their own characteristics, Eddie never forgot the joy of that first impression.

For her part, Maureen always chuckled at the memory of the rather frightening and eccentrically dressed figure (Eddie had been wearing a thick brown working drape, black drains, and crepe soles with leather uppers) that had suddenly bellowed with laughter in that black hole, with all its unpleasant connotations, while all around him the daffodils and primroses were flowering in the bright spring sunshine.

Two months after they met, Maureen and the twins moved into the Mansions with Eddie.

Three months after they met, Eddie told Maureen that he'd hang up his drapes when he reached the age of thirty-eight.

'Not for me, you won't,' Maureen responded sharply. Then, after a pause: 'You do what you want love, but don't do anything you'll regret, especially if you think you're doin' it for me. You'll end up blamin' me, or if not me, my stepdad, or your dad, or maybe all of us. It may sound corny and all that, but I love you as you are—that's the truth!'

But Eddie had made his decision and intended to stick to it, even though the consequences of it seemed too remote to worry about at the time.

*

Five years later, sitting beside the Limehouse basin, he realised that the decision, which had seemed easy and insignificant at the time would now be a hundred times more difficult. Being a Ted was his life, and he couldn't just pack it in like a bum job. Maureen had never been interested in the Ted scene—in fact, it left her cold. But she never once insisted, or even suggested that Eddie should pack it in, although she often secretly wished that Eddie would stay home and watch the telly with her and the twins more often.

To compound things, Maureen's stepfather had offered Eddie an assistant manager post in his surgical goods firm down at Bow. He had been gently putting the screws on Eddie to take it.

'But of course, the... er... gear,' he would gaze meaningfully at Eddie's drape jacket, 'would have to go, I'm afraid.'

'But I 'aven't sold a truss in my life,' said Eddie hopefully.

'No problem, John, no problem at all. Ten thousand a year, plus perks. The offer's open any time you want it, John, but I'm afraid the...er,' he made an expressive gesture at the back of his neck.

'Duck's arse,' said Eddie dryly.

'Whatever...' and Mr Turnbull of Turnbull's of Bow shook his head to indicate that a haircut would be an essential part of the deal.

'Think it over, son. Oh, you might find one of these comfortable,' said Mr Turnbull, playfully pushing the latest model of truss across his desk. Eddie bristled, sucking in his paunch, and Mr Turnbull cringed back in mock terror.

'Just a joke, John!'

This was the usual pattern of Eddie's interviews with Mr Turnbull.

Perhaps it was Maureen's generosity in not putting any pressure on him to change his lifestyle which had made Eddie feel guilty at the beginning, and which prompted him to make his rather self-centred promise. In a few weeks, Maureen had forgotten the promise and, even if she remembered what Eddie had said, she would never remind him of it or attempt to hold him to his word.

But Eddie never forgot.

Eddie shivered as the cold wind that had swept the clouds from the sky suddenly turned its attention to the land. A big bubble of methane welled up and burst at the point where the image of the jetliner had been, shattering the mirrored surface of the water, and Eddie looked round at the sound of a cry and loud splash from across the basin. He caught sight of something... something... something he couldn't quite make out, but something large and dark disappearing beneath the surface of the water, at the point where an eel fisherman's empty stool was sitting beside his glowing brazier.

'Fuck me!' he whispered, and a moment later he instinctively ducked and closed his eyes tight as a great shadow passed across the dark, jumbled fragments of the mirror, followed by a violent downdraft of air and a sound above as if a dozen large umbrellas had been rapidly opened and closed. The hairs on the back of Eddie's neck would have stood on end had they not been so weighed down with Trugel.

When Eddie opened his eyes again and looked up fearfully, there was nothing to be seen but a blue-black canopy, pricked with stars, which the last feeble glimmer of daylight could no longer conceal.

'Shhhhippam's Bloater Paste!' he breathed in awe.

*

A couple of hours earlier, just before Eddie began his perambulation along the canal, Pterry had made his customary swoop on the Evening News which old Mr

Caldecott always left on the bridge over the Hackney cut after his visit to the betting shop in Bladebone Lane. Now, he drummed on the newspaper with an agitated clawed digit, though a hint of amusement also lit up his ruby, lidless eyes as he read the headline.

"CONCRETE JUNGLE: URBAN LANDSCAPE IS NATURE'S NEW WILD.

By David Battenburg

Beneath the words were pictures of an alligator wandering across a golf course in Miami, a monitor lizard emerging from a toilet bowl in Bangkok, and a group of penguins riding on a bus in Cape Town.

Transparent membranes flicked across his eyes as he reached down with his long, pointed beak to turn to the next page, then the next with a deft twist of his neck. Occasionally he would pause and sigh, at the same time emitting a strange clicking sound as the very pronounced Adam's Apple in his scrawny neck came up to meet the goitrous appendage which hung below his beak. As he did this, he was swinging on a device a little like an acrobat's trapeze. Finally, despairing of finding anything else of interest, Pterry let the newspaper fall off his lap into the black abyss beneath him. Then at the last moment, something caught his eye and he lunged forward in an attempt to grab the paper – but it was too late. The glimmering white pages drifted down until they disappeared into the darkness. Pterry made an exasperated sucking sound. He spread his great wings and examined them in the light which filtered down from the circle of sky above him. Once he was content that they were in good order, he folded them around his small, pot-bellied body and dived down in pursuit of the newspaper.

It was a descent he had practiced many times before, opening his wings to break his fall at the last moment, before making a gentle landing on the chimney floor, which was now strewn with pages of newspaper. His eyes burned brightly in the gloom, and it wasn't long before he found the page he was looking for. He took it over to a pile of boxes which doubled as an armchair.

'**SIR GILES JELLICOE announces plans for Beckford regeneration**' read the headline: the clicking sounds in Pterry's gizzard began again as he read. 'Government minister announces **ISLE OF DOGS** to become the new City of London. Residents' protests threatened as talks begin with American multi-national MANDERVILLE HOLDINGS.'

Pterry's eyes blazed as he slowly and deliberately began to tear the page in half, then into quarters, eighths, and finally into tiny scraps of paper which he threw into the air. At the same time, with the sound of two giant umbrellas opening and closing, he beat his great wings so that his take off and rapid ascent left the scraps blowing about like confetti at a very strange wedding.

Chapter 4

Thinkin' About You

'Penny for 'em Eddie.'

Dolly Skeat's words made no impression on Eddie, who was staring intently at the rather moth-eaten kingfisher which shared a dirty, nicotine-stained glass case on the wall of The Bloody Mary's public bar with a pheasant. He might just as easily have been staring at the yellowing bream, the grinning pike, the tufted cockatoo, tiny goldcrest or any of the other fish and fowl which looked down on the drinkers from all parts of the bar. The kingfisher just happened to be directly opposite him, providing a mooring for his eyes while his imagination explored the events of the afternoon, particularly the big umbrellas which had scared the hell out of him.

Two Irishmen were leaning against the bar and pursuing a conversation in a low, almost continuous monotone in which individual words were indistinguishable, producing a sound Eddie found hypnotic, like a radio playing in another room.

'All right—tuppence for 'em then!'

This time Mrs Skeat's words, followed by a splutter of laughter from the Irishmen, had the effect of breaking the spell. Eddie reached for his pint.

'Sorry, Doll—miles away.'

He sipped sheepishly like a little boy who is up to no good but has been caught out. He coughed, knowing that Doll was still watching him, and whisked an imaginary speck of dust off his right drainpipe.

'You look a bit peaky, Eddie,' said Doll, cocking her head on one side, 'You all right?'

'Me? Yeah, fine, Doll—honest!'

Dolly Skeat knew Eddie and his moods better than most people. She had watched him grow up and seen many of his formative days and nights, sitting where he was sitting now. She narrowed her eyes and took a long look at Eddie as she methodically wiped and polished a glass which had been bone dry and shining for some minutes past.

'Come on, Eddie, what's up? It's not Maureen or the twins is it—they're not ill or anything?'

'Nah, they're fine, Doll—been down at West Ham this afternoon.'

'Then why are you looking so green round the gills—it's not my beer, I hope!' Doll pursed her lips and gave the glass in her hands an extra vigorous rub.

Eddie heaved a sigh and looked up at the ceiling where two silver paper 'goolies' (handmade silver paper darts with wet, chewed paper tips) were stuck fast.

'Doll, I know you're going to think I'm stupid or something, but...'

'I'm listening.'

'...Well, I think I saw something down at the Basin this afternoon.'

Doll stopped wiping the glass. 'Saw something?' she echoed.

'Well... not really saw... more heard... felt something...

44

can't quite explain.'

Doll banged the glass down on the draining board with an exasperated snort, making Eddie jump and temporarily silencing the two Irishmen. She put her hands on her hips.

'Edward Caldecott, you ought to be ashamed of yourself. Almost thirty-eight years old, and you're still running about by that filthy old canal like a schoolboy—small wonder it's finally turned you stupid. I...'

Eddie was saved from further chastisement by the appearance of Little Henry, who had been serving on the other side of the bar and had overheard the conversation. Henry was Doll's elder brother, a tiny man immaculately dressed in blue blazer and flannels, his grey hair slick and shiny on his head, his hands perfectly manicured. Doll towered above him like a kind of human beacon, streaks of her once red hair still glowing amongst billows of sandy grey curls. In spite of this, Henry had an immediately soothing effect on his sister.

'Evenin' Eddie,' said Henry.

'Evenin' 'Enery,' replied Eddie, relieved to see the little man.

'Doll been gettin' at you again, has she?' There was a hint of laughter in Henry's voice.

'Well, what's a grown man doin' runnin' about down by the canal?' asked Doll almost plaintively, her anger rapidly subsiding.

'What were thirty thousand grown men doing watchin' twenty-two other grown men running and swearing and rollin' in the mud down at Upton Park this afternoon, I'd like to know?' said Henry with great gravity. He fancied himself as a bit of a philosopher. Doll had no answer.

'That's different,' she said, sulkily lighting a cigarette

and busying herself down the other end of the bar.

Henry stood gazing out across the room, seeming to stare into space as Eddie had done a few minutes before.

'Is that you, Ollie?' he asked without turning his head.

'Indeed, it is Henry; I'll have two pints of Guinness when you're ready.'

Little Henry turned towards the two Irishmen. 'And Sean, too?'

'Good evening to you, Henry,' said Sean, 'and a box of matches for me.'

Ollie put the two empty glasses into Henry's outstretched hands. He turned, crossed to the other side of the bar, filled the two glasses, reached up for a box of matches and returned to the two Irishmen with scarcely a hesitation. Although he was completely blind, Henry was so familiar with the little world behind the bar that customers often came, were served, drank and went away again without ever realising his impediment. Two Smooves, young men with longish hair and moustaches, who had just come in certainly didn't guess the truth when Henry served them. They took their pints to a far corner and began to talk quietly in posh accents, occasionally stealing fascinated glances at Eddie and the stuffed creatures on the walls.

It was almost half past six by the old mantle clock above the bar, and Eddie was well aware that one of his mother's meat teas was waiting for him just down the road. He drained his glass and stood up.

'Cheerio then 'Enery... Doll.'

Dolly Skeat stubbed out her cigarette.

'O Rivoir Edward,' said Henry raising his hand, 'Give our love to Albert and Ethel.'

Doll smiled. 'I love's you really, Eddie,' she said in a

hoarse voice, blowing out a cloud of smoke as she spoke, 'but no more close encounters—please!' Eddie chuckled, opened the door and was about to go out when Henry called after him. 'I've felt those things too Eddie—go careful, son.'

*

In Paragon Road, the mist had thickened into a fog: Eddie could hardly make out the lights of the Mansions as he made his way towards No. 91. He reached the Velox, and looked her over with concern; then, having made sure that no acts of vandalism had been perpetrated, he gave her boot an appreciative pat. Maureen wasn't keen on having her bottom patted, so Eddie reserved this expression of affection exclusively for the Velox.

Just before he reached No. 91's neatly clipped privet hedge, he fancied that he heard the umbrella sound again, only this time it was far, far above him. He stood still, held his breath and listened, but there was nothing. Even so, he felt the hairs making another attempt to stand up on the back of his neck and he broke into a run. Once he reached the crazy-paved sanctuary of his parents' front garden, he stopped and composed himself. Two severely pruned rose trees stood stiffly to attention, seeming to upbraid him for being a coward. He took out a handkerchief, mopped his forehead, straightened his bootlace tie and raised the brass galleon door knocker, but before he could bring it down the door opened.

'Oh, Blimey!'

'Dad,' Eddie nodded to his father as he pushed past him in the narrow hall.

'Albert, is that Ted? Is that you Ted?' piped Ethel's voice

from the dining room. Eddie entered the little room and went over to his mother who had screwed up her eyes and held up her face for the ritual kiss to be bestowed.

'Hello, Mum,' said Eddie as he delivered a real smacker to Ethel's cheek, making her wince.

'You must be hungry after your walk, Ted,' said Ethel, 'You look rather pale—you're not sickening for something are you?'

'Yeah, wouldn't surprise me at all if he hasn't caught malaria wandering about by that bleedin' drain,' interjected his father as he set about creating an enormous, corned beef and ham sandwich.

The table was laid with an ornate pink china tea service, the centrepiece of which was a large platter on which slices of corned beef, spam and liver sausage reclined on a bed of lettuce; another smaller plate bore a great number of heavily buttered slices of Mother's Pride bread. Standing between the plates were two pots of SHIPPAM'S BLOATER PASTE. The sight of this 'cold collation' combined with the peculiar smell in the room—a mixture of cooking, Papworth the cat, musty furniture and possibly something beneath the floor boards— made Eddie feel slightly nauseous.

'Come on, Ted, don't wait for me,' said Ethel pouring the tea.

Eddie sniffed the air cautiously. There wasn't anything on the table which immediately recommended itself to his palate.

'Has Papworth done naughties in here recently?' he asked, wrinkling his nose. Mrs Caldecott looked pained.

'No, she has not,' she said, 'she's a very good old girl— and I don't know why you insist on calling her...THAT name, when you know her name's Tina.'

At that moment, a moth-eaten, guilty-looking marmalade cat emerged from behind the armchair in the corner and hobbled out into the kitchen. It was the twins who had christened her Papworth, not because they thought she might benefit from a heart transplant, but merely because they had heard the name on the news and liked the sound of it. Eddie agreed with the twins that it suited the cat—and he couldn't resist teasing his mother.

'I didn't mean it, Mum,' he said, flinging a huge paw around her and making her spill the tea.

'Ooooh, Ted—now look what you've made me do,' she said, pushing him away.

Old Mr Caldecott had chomped his way through this exchange between his wife and son; now he wiped his bristly moustache and began to construct another sandwich.

'You wouldn't credit it for the time of year, Eth,' he said reaching for another slice of Spam, 'but Diana Dors has still got two lovely blooms and I can't bring myself to prune her.'

'Go on, Dad, give her the chop—she's well past it now,' said Eddie digging a playful elbow into his father's ribs.

Mr C. sniffed contemptuously. 'Hignoremus,' he said, biting into his second sandwich. He was a fanatical rose grower, his back garden a parade ground where a beautifully turned-out company was drawn up in weed-free, well-mulched beds. This was all in stark contrast to the writhing, tangled mass in No. 93's garden next door. It was a constant source of pain to Albert Caldecott that his new neighbours, ageing-hippies Roderick and Natasha Venables, should favour the 'romantic wilderness' approach to gardening. He had tried, without success, to convince them of the importance of weeding, spraying, hoeing, pelleting, dead-heading and pruning, with the result that he was almost helpless to prevent a huge army of bugs, slugs and snails from crawling, slithering and humming forth every evening to try their luck on his minefields of Slug Death and insecticide. Many would die, but some would inevitably get through to gorge themselves before retreating to their jungle hideouts at dawn; it was Mr Caldecott's own private little Vietnam.

One day Albert had decided to gamble on a last desperate stratagem. He had recruited the services of the Venables children, two filthy-faced golden-haired little angels named Benedict and Gwendoline. Offering them a new halfpenny for every dandelion head, slug, snail or caterpillar, and 2p for every matchbox full of greenfly captured in their parents' garden, he had set his two little scalp hunters to work, making them swear to secrecy. It had only been after parting with a fiver in exchange for ten repulsive carrier bags full of carnage that he had caught Ben and Gwen red-handed, sneaking back from the Hackney Marshes with bulging bags. He had threatened them, cajoled them, and finally begged them for his money. But there was nothing he had been able to do about it—they had known they had him over a barrel and had threatened to reveal his whole sordid scheme to their parents. So once again, the dandelions flowered and sent countless parachutist seeds floating with the aphids across the fence into Mr C's plot, while beneath them the land force threw themselves with gay abandon upon Slug Death and tender rose shoots alike.

'Imagine a wide boy like me falling for an old trick like that,' Albert sighed, his head in his hands, having just recounted the story yet again to Eddie and Ethel.

'Wide boy,' said Ethel, 'I've never found you very wide dear—quite easy to get round, in fact.' Ethel didn't often make jokes, but she was pleased with this one. Old Mr Caldecott squeezed his wife's hand, feeling comforted in adversity, and resigned himself to the fact that the Venables jungle wouldn't go away.

Eddie pushed away his plate with a mock sigh of satisfaction and stood up. 'Thanks, Mother, that was t'riffic.'

A look of pained bewilderment once more clouded Ethel's face as she stared at the half-eaten sandwich on Eddie's plate, then up at her son, then back at the Spam sandwich again.

'But you haven't finished, Ted—you sure you're not ill?'

'Course he's bleeding well ill,' said old Mr Caldecott biting into his third sandwich. 'Give him some bloater paste—that'll sort him out.'

'No, honest, Mum, I couldn't eat any more—Dad'll finish it, won't you?' said Eddie, patting his father lightly on the shoulder.

'What—and catch bleeding swamp fever? You must be joking mate,' said Mr C. through a mouthful of corned beef.

'Bye, Dad,' said Eddie, walking out into the hall with Ethel fussing along behind him.

'Love to Maureen,' she said at the door.

'When are you going to marry that lovely girl, eh?' came old Mr Caldecott's voice from the dining room.

'Don't pay him any mind, Ted. Oh… almost forgot,' said Ethel, bustling off and coming back a moment later with two large bars of chocolate. 'For Ronnie and Derek.' she said, slipping them into the pocket of Eddie's drape.

'Thanks, Mum,' said Eddie, bending to kiss his mother, who screwed up her eyes and offered a cheek once more, though this time Eddie didn't deliver a smacker, just a light peck on the forehead. As he did so, he noticed with shock how thin and drawn she had become over the last few weeks. Ethel had been ill in the summer and had lost a lot of weight, though when she had recovered, she had seemed at first to be looking better for it, having been fairly portly before. But now the skin was stretched over her skull, her usually lustrous white hair seemed thin and lifeless, and dark patches had appeared under her eyes, which had lost some of their sparkle.

'You all right, Mum?' asked Eddie. 'You don't look too clever.'

Ethel Caldecott tutted and turned away. 'Me? I'm right as rain—just a bit tired, that's all. You're a fine one to talk, anyway, coming in looking like you've seen a ghost, then not finishing your tea! Humph!'

'Look after yourself, Mum, won't you?' said Eddie, squeezing her frail hands before turning to go. At the gate, he looked back and saw her still standing in the doorway, silhouetted by the light in the hall.

'Bye 'bye blackbird,' she said, giving a little wave before going back inside and closing the door.

At that moment, Eddie would have given anything to have turned the clock back an hour, to have raised the galleon door knocker again and to have gone into that little kitchen parlour and eaten three or four spam and corn beef sandwiches, all the while keeping an expression on his face as if he was sampling the finest caviar. He hesitated, tears welling up in his eyes, but it was too late. Instead, he glanced up nervously into the foggy night sky, then turned up the collar of his drape and set off towards the Mansions.

Chapter 5

I'm Ready

If an angel—or any other large, winged creature such as a Pteranodon from the Upper Cretaceous period—had passed high overhead that Saturday night, Beckford would have looked to them like a city under the sea, its lights suffusing the milky waters which covered even the tallest tower block ten fathoms deep. Swooping down, our angel might have hovered just above the surface of the fog and been able to make out individual lights directly below, some gliding along like the headlights of the Velox, others motionless like the Caldecotts' porch light, soon to go out, or the neon sign outside The Happy Sole Fish Bar in Beckford High Street. Perhaps some muffled sounds would have floated up from below, the clash of goods trucks in the great marshalling yards, or the brief crescendo of an ambulance siren. Inquisitive to know what sort of creatures might live on the floor of this strange ocean, our angel might have swept back his great leathery wings and plunged into the luminous vapour before spreading them again to glide down in a gentle arc, alighting at last on the forbidding bulk of the United Reform Church in Penrose Avenue. From there our angel would have caught a whiff of the evening fry-up and prompted by a gurgling stomach, flapped quietly across

Beckford High Street and come to rest on the roof of The Happy Sole. Folding his wings, he might have crept quietly to the parapet and peered down into the street where he would have seen two brightly coloured creatures eating the source of the stomach-rumbling smell out of old newspapers.

As he watched, he would have seen other creatures coming in and out of the shop below or walking along the pavement. These were similar to the brightly coloured ones, but drab by comparison, lacking the shiny horns on their foreheads, or the thin legs, flashing ankles and enormous feet which were among the salient features of the brightly coloured ones.

After a while, a door opened in the building opposite and three more brightly coloured, big-footed ones emerged, accompanied by a brief fanfare of music. They swished across the street and went into the shop below; then the two brightly coloured ones who had been eating crossed the street in the opposite direction. They went in through the same door and were greeted by a similar burst of music. Intrigued, our angel might have strained his eyes to read the faded lettering above the door. And when he did finally manage to decipher the words, he might have found that they had a strangely familiar ring about them, which touched a chord deep down in his eternity of memories—*SAMSON AND DELILAH.*

Just as the coming and going of a few gaudy wasps betrays the presence of their nest nearby, so the knots of Teds inside The Happy Sole or leaning up against lampposts on the pavement were the only indication that The Samson and Delilah was anything other than the small, grimy local which it looked like from the street. There were no bright lights or billboards outside, while thick velvet curtains blocked views

54

of the interior and two sets of double doors muffled the sounds.

That Saturday night, the two long-haired Smooves who had stared at Eddie with such undisguised curiosity in The Bloody Mary tried to peer inside but failed. They held a whispered conference, glancing nervously across at the Teds in front of The Happy Sole, then slipped furtively through the first set of doors. They hesitated for a moment in the gloomy airlock inside; then, summoning up courage, they pushed open the second set of doors and flinched involuntarily as the atmosphere which filled the room was sucked past them like a rush of escaping gas.

Shading their eyes against the glare, they had time to catch a glimpse of garishly dressed, elaborately coiffured creatures moving through a thick, steamy haze against a patterned background of writhing tendrils which decorated the wall paper on every side and disappeared into the shadows beyond the great, yellow globes of light which hung over the exotic scene like moons above a jungle clearing on some far away fantastic planet.

'Sorry, gents, no 'taches tonight.'

The sharp voice brought the Smooves back to reality with a jerk; they fingered their hairy upper lips nervously as they found themselves facing 'Spotted' Dick Beeson, a scrawny Ted dressed in a leopard skin suit and corduroy/check flat cap or 'ratter.' He was sitting at the small table immediately facing the door where he collected admission money and earned himself his other nickname of 'Tax Gatherer.' He looked so frightening that the Smooves were starting to turn, to leave in blind panic, when Dick called them back.

'Pahnd 'n'arf each then lads—but keep off the dance floor,' he said, as if he was doing them a favour by charging them three times the normal admission price. The Smooves thanked him profusely and gave the impression, as they fished out their cash, that they would willingly have parted with much larger sums for the privilege of spending an evening in the Samson without forfeiting their moustaches.

It was only half past eight, and as the ripped off Smooves were making their way timidly towards the bar, the Hepcats, who were headlining that night, had just begun to set up their equipment. Stan Burnette, a short, stout bespectacled Ted, was doing brisk business at his Rollin' Wax vintage record stall. Stan had changed his name by deed poll from Pope to Burnette in honour of the legendary Johnny Burnette. He was also known as The Ubangi Man because of his collection of all known versions of the Rock 'n Roll classic *Ubangi Stomp*—there were fifty-seven in all.

Across the room, DJ Cadillac Jack sat in a pool of light on his own personal dais, sequin drape glittering, bow wave fresh out of curlers and coiled on top of his head like a dark, shiny Danish pastry. He slapped an old Gene Vincent number on the turntable, enticing two young Teds who were long in the quiff but smooth of cheek onto the floor, and also a dapper old black guy in a white baggy suit and fedora. The two Teds, frowning with concentration, began a furious toe and heel bop interspersed with the occasional clinically executed back-flip or press-up, plunging to the floor, hands outstretched, then springing up effortlessly, flipping over in mid-air and going down again to repeat the manoeuvre on their backs. These fledgling Teds, self-conscious in their bright new drapes, performed their routine with an unsmiling, mechanical expertise which would have earned them high marks for technical merit but little for artistic interpretation. By contrast, the old black guy pirouetted slowly and gracefully, his creased face cracked into a permanent smile, his arm crooked as if to steer an imaginary partner around the floor.

Naz and Ken (Nasir and Kenji), two Teds from Bangladesh and Japan respectively, looked on from a corner of the dance floor, soberly and immaculately dressed in grey drapes and dark blue crepes. The quality of their jet-black hair—particularly Ken's—allowed for the sculpting of gravity-defying quiffs. Naz and Ken never danced, never smiled, and cultivated an air of mystery and aloofness, communicating only through a slight tilt of the head, sway of the quiff or raise of an eyebrow. That generally suited Eddie just fine as he was a man of few words.

When the man himself made his entry, heads turned, quiffs wobbled, and even the dancers missed a step. Eddie had changed out of his powder blue drape into his dress suit, the pride of his wardrobe, a threadbare, charcoal grey number with a black velvet collar made at Busberry's of Romford in 1960. Nothing flash, but still very sharp indeed, it marked him out as a true original; a pair of enormous crepe-soled brothel creepers replaced the winklepickers, spreading out beneath his spindly ankles like divers' boots, making him seem less top heavy than when he was wearing the 'winks.'

'There you are, my son,' he said, dropping a 10p piece into Dick Beeson's cash box and patting him on the ratter before moving over to the bar.

Eddie had savoured this moment and experienced the exhilaration of arrival a thousand times before, but he had never felt more at ease in that familiar setting—or more relieved, in a strange way, by what he saw around him. Though it was only three days since his last session in the Samson, he was feeling like a traveller who, while wandering in some distant land, hears a rumour that his home town has been devastated by an earthquake and comes rushing back, only to find that the rumours were false and that life continues very much as he had always known it, on the surface at least.

'Some kind-a earthquake,' whispered Eddie as he leaned back against the bar and surveyed the scene before him; then a thin voice piped up beside him:

'Shorry about Thurshday night, Eddie, I was going to come in, but I had thish 'flu, like, and me mum wouldn't let me out of the house, otherweish I'd've...'

The voice was cut off in mid-flow as Eddie turned around, a broad grin of recognition on his face, and threw an enormous paw around the speaker's coat-hanger shoulders.

'And how's my little ray of con'inen'al sunshine then? I've mished you shorely, Shpider, my shun, but you shound bleedin' rough—perhapsh I should take you back to your muvver?'

'Leave it out will 'ya?' squeaked Spider in intense embarrassment, struggling to extricate his weedy frame from Eddie's bearhug embrace.

Spider Spinetti was the youngest and scrawniest of a family of seven. His parents had come over from Italy in 1958, hoping to make their fortune; nineteen years later, they were still sweating it out in their dry-cleaning business in Dalston Lane. Spider had grown up in that hissing, steaming, crumpled and creased little world. Some of his earliest memories were of Teds bringing their gear in to be cleaned, and of gazing in wonder at the freshly laundered drapes, glowing like precious stones among the other drab and tawdry garments which hung on the collection rack.

Another of Spider's early memories was of tinkering. As soon as he could wield a screwdriver, he had set about every household item he could lay his hands on that contained some sort of mechanism—clocks, radios, hairdryers, the telly—all had been opened up, observed closely, then put back together again, usually in the right order. As he had grown older, he had begun to focus his attention on the ultimate tinkering object—the motor car. By the time he had left school at the age of sixteen, he had been able to strip down almost any car engine you cared to name. He worked half the week in the dry-cleaning shop, and half with his uncle Bruno in Rizla's garage under the railway arches in Beckford. After a month or two he had saved enough to buy himself a fingertip, box-backed, bottle green drape and he was ready for the Samson.

'Spider, my old son, I was all right as it happens,' said Eddie, adopting a rather injured tone of voice and removing his arm from Spider's coat hanger shoulders. 'Lucky the Old Bill didn't wish me goodnight, mind,' he continued, 'otherwise old Uncle Eddie really would have been in shtook. Still, that's what happens when you come to depend, I s'pose—too much to ask of your mates nowadays. Would it be too much of an imposition to ask you to take me and her home tonight?' said Eddie, clasping his hands together in a beseeching gesture.

'Corsh not,' said Spider, sniffing and looking sheepish, 'like I said it was me mum who…'

'Come on then, I'll buy you a lemonade,' said Eddie, hanging his arm on the coat hanger again and drawing the chastened Spider towards the bar.

Spider idolised Eddie. For the last couple of years, he had acted almost as his personal chauffeur, driving him in the Velox between the Mansions and the Samson, and occasionally taking him and Maureen down to Southend or Littlehampton on bank holiday weekends and other official joyride days in the Teds' calendar. At the end of those outings, he would always drive the Velox back to her garage beneath the railway arches at Beckford where he would lovingly attend to her every need, making sure she was in peak condition for her next appearance. Spider still remembered his first night in the Samson with pride. Eddie had come to his rescue when two or three older Teds had accused him of being a 'plastic' because of his age and the bright new drapes he wore.

'Who's callin' who a 'plastic' then?' Eddie had asked in his most menacing voice as he pushed aside Spider's tormentors. 'An' I s'pose you powder puffs think you're 'originals' an' all, don'tcha, just because you're a bit long in the tooth and you're wearing crumby old drapes. Look at that,' he said, turning one of the Teds around, 'that's not a drape, it's a converted overcoat with a bleedin' great seam down the back. You need to see a tailor, my son,' he said, shoving 'converted overcoat', into the arms of his mates. They hadn't had the stomach to argue with Eddie, so had mooched off to the other end of the bar and started playing pinball.

Eddie had hung his arm on Spider's coat hanger for the first time that night and had given him a piece of wisdom—

an honour he did not often confer. 'Listen my son, it's not age or old drapes that make you a real Ted, it's commitment— you live the life all day and every day, and none of them powder puffs will be able to say you ain't a real Ted.'

Spider remembered those words through the dullness of his cold on that Saturday night two years later and felt a little ashamed that he had let Eddie down, even ever so slightly by staying home in bed. He would never have dreamed that Eddie also remembered those words that night, and that he too felt ashamed, though for quite different reasons.

It was from that point in the evening that Eddie's mood began to turn sour. As he watched his pint being poured, his thoughts turned back to the events of the afternoon, and the depressing prospect of his thirty-eighth birthday, with all its implications. He looked at Spider and wondered how he would ever be able to face him again after all he had told him about commitment.

The Hepcats began to play Carl Perkins' 'Matchbox,' and most of the other Teds, including Spider, gathered round the stage, but Eddie remained leaning against the bar, staring into his beer and watching little bubbles forming into clusters on the surface before bursting or drifting to the edge of the glass and merging with the ring of white froth which floated there. Every now and again, he would tip the whole lot down his throat and order a fresh pint. He was beginning to feel like a man who has been told he only has six months to live and whose appreciation of life is, at one moment, suddenly heightened, so that he revels in all its richness and variety, but then in the next moment his realisation that it will all be gone soon makes that same life feel like a grey, meaningless monotony, relieved only by the occasional knot of sadness or hardship.

The sound of the Hepcats was making him rediscover his loathing of rockabilly, and the drink wasn't doing much to prevent his continuing slide into gloom—in fact, it was lubricating the slippery slope. He looked round for sympathetic spirits and saw Willie the Wig standing at the far end of the bar with Dotun and Delroy, two huge Teds of African and West Indian heritage respectively, who always wore leopard skin ratters and drapes three-buttoned across their barrel chests. Willie put his hand to the back of his neck and tilted his toupee bow wave in Eddie's direction by way of greeting. Eddie nodded back and began to saunter towards them with the intention of having a group moan when a great wave of apathy overtook and washed over him—why bother? In a few months' time, he wouldn't be giving a damn if the Samson had been reduced to rubble and Eddie Cochran had never been born, so what was the point about grumbling over Rockabilly now? He walked straight past Willie, Dotun and Delroy into the street.

Outside, activity was at a minimum. The Happy Sole was empty, only the occasional car floated past in the fog. The city was experiencing that curious lull before the pubs and entertainments turn out their customers.

Eddie felt as if he was in a dream as he crossed the street and went into the chip shop. It wasn't just the drink and the weight of his crepe boppers which made his limbs heavy and his movements mechanical. It was as if some life force had drained out of him.

Behind the counter a short, swarthy man slid off his stool and walked up briskly to serve Eddie. Every part of his body seemed to glisten with oil.

'Usual, Eddie?' he asked, cocking his head on one side, eyes twinkling. Eddie nodded.

Mr Akrawi, the proprietor of The Happy Sole, dextrously began to prepare a steak and kidney pie and chips, folding the newspaper with a few bold, origami strokes before presenting a perfect inverted paper volcano full of steaming food.

'Wassamatta, Eddie, you look like maybe you've seen a ghost. Don't like the music tonight?'

Eddie thought about the shadow on the water and the rushing wind down by the Limehouse Basin and nodded. Then he thought about the Hepcats, frowned and shook his head.

'Ha, I don't blame you,' said Mr Akrawi, somewhat confused, 'these noises, they are not my cup of tea.'

As Mr Akrawi was speaking, Eddie saw a frown appear on his normally jovial face as the door opened behind him. Without turning round, Eddie watched the reflection of the new customer in the burnished metal of the deep fryer, and even though the image was distorted, he recognised the uniform at once, the green bomber jacket and shaven skull of a skinhead. A dent in the deep fryer lid extended the skin's skull to almost alien proportions and made a crooked scar of his mouth. The scar split into an open wound and spoke.

'Fuck me if it ain't the Golden Age of Rock 'n Roll. Too crocked to rock, is it Grandad?'

Eddie said nothing, didn't turn around, just watched the skinhead's reflection in the fryer. The scar split again.

'Sav'loy and chips.'

Mr Akrawi would have liked to have told the skinhead to get out of his shop. But he was wise enough to realise the consequences of such a course of action—daubings on the walls outside, broken windows, maybe even a roughing up down some dark alley, so he slowly prepared the food and handed it over. But the skinhead wasn't satisfied.

'Oi, dago man, this ain't a full portion of chips! Look'a'that, call that twenty bleedin' pence worth? Gimme some more!'

'Is a full portion of chips,' said Mr Akrawi, trying to keep calm, and somewhat reassured by Eddie's presence in his shop.

The skinhead's face turned bright red and seemed to inflate with anger. The next moment he threw the chips into the air, and they fell like autumn leaves, one of them lodging on the remains of Eddie's bow wave. Very slowly Eddie retrieved the chip from its resting place and turned round, chip in hand.

'Look sonny, I know you grapefruits ain't too clever, but you can understand English can't cha? The man said it's a full portion of chips and that's what it is, so take this, pick the rest of 'em up and fuck right along out of 'ere.'

For a moment, the protagonists confronted one another, faces no more than an inch apart before the skinhead turned on his heel and almost ran out of The Happy Sole. But he was gone for only a few moments. As Eddie calmly resumed eating, the skin reappeared, grabbed the salt bottle which always stood on the shelf by the doorway, and with a horrid yell, threw it at Eddie who ducked. The salt bottle hit Mr Akrawi on his bald pate, but luckily glanced off that glistening hemisphere like shrapnel off a tin hat. However, the blow was still enough to send him to the floor.

Roaring with rage and spitting chips, Eddie charged out in pursuit, holding his paper cone before him like an Olympic torch. But what he found in the street made his roar die into a whisper which ended in a single, almost soundless, mouthed expletive.

'Shippam's!'

Six of the meanest looking skins he had ever seen stood facing him on the damp, neon-lit pavement. Eddie glanced quickly at the *Samson*, but there wasn't a Ted in sight, so he took a deep breath and a firm grip on his steaming pie and chips. The biggest skin was already slouching forward. Eddie immediately recognised him from past encounters—Goliath. White scars ran across his skull like lines of chalk on a freshly burned stubble field, and on his battered forehead a swastika and the letters N.F. were crudely tattooed in red.

'Remember me, Teddy Bear?'

Eddie did not reply.

'Oi—BALDECOTT—I remember you.'

'No, sorry, can't say I remember you,' said Eddie without a tremor in his voice, 'but then again you grapefruits are all the same, ain't cha? Six for 50p down Ridley Road ain't it?'

With a howl Goliath lunged forward, grabbed Eddie by the lapels of his drape and drew back his grizzly head ready to 'nut' his adversary.

Now, Eddie never looked for trouble but, being a Ted, and a well-known one at that, he had come to expect it, and that was why Goliath never completed his nutting, but instead let out a shrill scream of pain as the barbless fishhooks sewn under Eddie's lapels pierced his fingers. A moment later, the scream ceased abruptly, and was replaced by a sharp inhalation denoting even greater agony as Eddie brought his heavy crepe bopper smartly up between Goliath's legs, doubling him up and thus presenting an unprotected cranium on which Eddie crammed his pie and chips, the paper cone sticking up for a moment like a dunce's cap before Eddie brought his clenched fist down, crushing the cone, bursting the pie and sending a gout of black, boiling gravy onto the bare skin beneath. With a dismal moan, Goliath sank to his knees before toppling over onto his side.

The remaining skinheads hesitated for a moment when they saw Goliath, their leader, vanquished so quickly and so completely. In fact, they were on the point of beating a retreat until fate, in the form of a large, soft dog turd, intervened between the crepe sole of Eddie's left bopper and the slippery pavement, causing him to lose his footing and stagger backwards. At once the skins were on him like a pack of wolves, knocking off his shades and crushing them beneath large bovver boots. Almost blind, Eddie lashed out wildly at the blur of shapes which surrounded him. Two of his haymakers connected satisfyingly with a stubbly chin, but it was an unequal struggle and soon he was down and concentrating on protecting his balls as best he could.

Curiously enough, Eddie didn't feel much pain at first when the boots went in, partly because of the quantity of beer he had consumed, but mainly because he suddenly found himself in a state bordering on euphoria. It was as if his mind had become completely relaxed, had ceased to grapple with the vexing problems which had been troubling it all day and had said to his body, 'all right, now it's your turn to take the knocks for a while.'

Like a drowning man who has given up the struggle for life, he sank dreamily towards unconsciousness, reflecting with a smile that while it wouldn't be a truly romantic death in the James Dean tradition, this was at least better than the languid drift into night, which he had been picturing for himself after his thirty-eighth birthday. Then, just before blackness engulfed him, he thought of Maureen and the twins for the first time. Immediately, his whole body was filled with the most excruciating pain, and he became intensely aware of the aching spot at which each kick had landed. The taste of blood in his mouth and the stench of dog shit somewhere near his face made him want to retch violently. So far, he hadn't made a sound other than the occasional involuntary expulsion of air during the few seconds that the grubby battle had lasted, but now he rolled over onto his back, and let out a great bellow of pain which sent a fountain of blood into the air. A moment later Spider appeared at the door of the *Samson*, ducked back inside for a second, then reappeared with Naz 'n Ken, Dotun, Delroy and Willie the Wig at his heels.

The skinheads stayed around long enough to be baffled by Naz 'n Ken's martial arts moves, for Delroy to knock a couple of bald skulls together and for Willie to lose his luxuriant toupé to a startled opponent who immediately paid for his discovery with a flattened nose. Meanwhile, Spider was taking the first steps towards putting Eddie back together again, while Mr Akrawi, who had recovered from his encounter with the salt bottle, danced up and down in the doorway of his shop before offering 'As much as you can eat boys!' to the rescue party.

*

Maureen could have been a lot angrier with Eddie than she

was when they finally got him back to the Mansions. When she had satisfied herself that his injuries were no worse than a few cuts and many bruises, she confined herself to a 'you fuckin' arsehole,' then set about the business of soothing and dabbing him to sleep.

What worried her more deeply than Eddie's injuries was the fact that he had clearly been brooding about something for months and she couldn't tell what it was. What she did know from past experience was that he would have to be left to work it out for himself. For his part, Eddie felt that his problems had in some way been solved by the events of the night, though all that had really happened was that his determination to hang up his drapes and crepes had been strengthened. Meanwhile, the twins were fascinated by the spectacle of the blood-spattered Eddie lying on the bed, and looked on with ghoulish fascination, clamouring for the full details of the brawl until the bedroom door was finally locked against them.

For the time being, Eddie felt content and at peace, and though his body ached all over, nowhere was the pain so severe as to be unbearable. The swellings and bruises were still fresh and hadn't yet become excruciatingly tender while his joints hadn't yet stiffened to make any movement an agony.

He normally wore flannelette pyjamas every night, summer and winter, so the novelty of his nakedness and the constant dabbing and rubbings of ointment was arousing his carnal appetite. And on the spiritual side, he had never felt more loving towards Maureen or so grateful for her companionship. The result was that after a particularly titillating application of witch hazel, the nurse found herself the object of as passionate an advance as her patient's body would allow. Athletic it wasn't, but there could be no doubt that they weren't making anything else but love. In time-honoured fashion, their two hearts beat as one, like a pair of giant wings high up in the November night over slumbering Beckford.

Chapter 6

Three Steps to Heaven

Maureen stood in her bedroom at the top of the Mansions and stared out of the window into the bright morning. She was smiling because it was a long time since she had last felt so happy. She felt like she was swelling with joy, and she was determined not to let anything darken her mood.

It was over two months since Eddie's fight and most of his injuries had healed, though a broken nose and a broken front tooth (which Eddie had insisted should not be repaired) hadn't left him looking any prettier. Maureen had taken to calling him the Creature from the Black Lagoon, but she wasn't really worried by his appearance. Eddie had never been much of a dreamboat, certainly not over the last ten years, so that morning she laughed out loud at the memory of how he had worn his injuries like a ten-year-old as he propped up the bar in the *Samson* before Christmas.

The doctors had discovered that he had in fact cracked a couple of ribs, so he was given a plaster barrel to wear round his chest which, when covered somewhat awkwardly with a hastily modified waistcoat and drape, gave him a monstrously awe-inspiring appearance which was highlighted by his chipped front tooth. The twins thought he made a perfect Incredible Hulk.

But that morning it wasn't just the memory of Eddie's appearance which had made Maureen laugh so spontaneously, it was also the joy she had been finding in Eddie's reborn relish for life. Ever since that night in November, he had seemed like a new man. The mood of depression which had hung about him for so long had been blown away like an autumn mist.

Maureen was watching the twins booting a football around on the estate far below. She could hardly believe how tall Ronnie had grown over the past year. In their games of football, he was always the goalkeeper. He was being busily assailed by Derek like a cornstalk being circled by an angry wasp. On another day, the sight of them might have made Maureen feel old, but today it inspired her with new life and energy. The mud patch over which the twins were slipping, and sliding was covered with the slushy remains of the previous night's snowfall. Maureen was still suffering from the residue of a cold, so in other circumstances she might not have been relishing an afternoon on the terraces at Upton Park. But today she wouldn't have disappointed the twins for the world, and she knew she would probably come away feeling pleased that she had made the effort. Besides which, the Hammers were in good form so it would hopefully be a decent game. Ron slipped and went down on his bottom as Derek kicked the ball over him and raised his clenched fists in the air to acknowledge the silent roar from the terraces.

Maureen looked up from the little Cup Final with a new smile on her face. London, which so often felt overwhelmingly vast, was today a toy town for her to play with. She fixed her eyes on the pale, thin spire, no bigger than an ice cream cone dropped in the grass, which stuck up from the patch of smudgy tones that was Beckford cemetery in the middle distance of the scene before her. Closing her eyes, she imagined Eddie in the shadow of the gothic chapel, up to his ears in a grave, with daffodils flowering all around, as he had been on the day when she first met him. She laughed out loud at the memory of Eddie's face earlier in the week when he had asked her to marry him and she had answered 'Ta very much, thought you'd never ask,' secretly thinking he was a pig to have waited ten years to pop the question. She had almost been able to hear the air escaping from Eddie as he had deflated like a punctured lilo, but she'd had the heart to put the bung back in him with a big hug and a whispered, 'You make me very happy.' It made her happier still that he had asked her before knowing about her pregnancy, which had been confirmed at the doctor's that morning.

*

In reality, only plastic tulips were blooming in Beckford cemetery that day. The daffodils had hardly stirred from their bulbs, and those which had dared to peep above ground were covered by a shroud of snow which lay almost as deep and undisturbed as the dead.

Only the broader avenues and paths in the cemetery were regularly mown and tended. A smooth carpet of snow lay on them. Elsewhere—except where living relations still ministered to their dead—grasses, brambles, wild flowers of every kind and a host of saplings had grown up unchecked. Gravestones and crosses pushed their way up through this underbrush like toadstools on a forest floor. The grandiose columns and the occasional mausoleum bore witness to a more prosperous period in Beckford's history. Unknown to most of the inhabitants of the borough, prosperity of a sort was soon to come again, prosperity for which many of both the living and dead would have to make way. Stone angels perched on many of the larger monuments, some with wings outspread, others with feathers neatly folded on their backs, but each one sporting a fur hat of snow and a scarf to match. A few lay covered in white, like corpses in a field hospital, their foundations undermined by tiny seeds, which had burst open the graves into which they had fallen as they grew from saplings into trees.

It was only three o'clock in the afternoon, but the sun was low in the sky and the trees and saplings had grown so thick that most of the graveyard was already in shadow, except where a few stray shafts managed to pierce the lattice work of branches to light an angel's face here or an illegible epitaph there. Only the tops of the taller trees and the spire of the gothic chapel were still bright with sunlight, but countless snow crystals on the ground reflected the brilliant colour of the sky above, giving a tinge of blue to even the darkest shadows beneath laden branches.

In the centre of the cemetery, there was a small open space, not much more than a clearing in the woods, where the Victorian gothic chapel stood uncertainly with its superfluous turrets and minarets. Lit by the curious oblique light, it seemed as if it had just materialised, and would vanish as soon as its observer turned away, like a fairy tale castle. Though its lower windows had been boarded up, the structure hadn't been damaged or changed in any way other than by the slow erosion of nature. Vandals hadn't left their mark there or in any other part of the cemetery. The youth of Beckford seemed to be possessed of a kind of dread of the place, or perhaps they simply had no quarrel with this period of their country's architectural heritage, preferring to wreak their vengeance on the anonymous tower blocks and housing estates which had sprung up after the old Victorian and Edwardian terraces had been ploughed into the ground.

On most days, the living sounds of the city would just be audible to someone standing near the chapel in the clearing. However, on this afternoon even that low groundswell of sound was muffled by the snow, so that in spite of the millions of people surrounding that spot on the A-Z map, the clearing might just as easily have been somewhere in the Black Forest rather than in the middle of London.

From a distance the dark, moving shape at the edge of the clearing could have been mistaken for a large, low-slung animal rooting around for food in the undergrowth, but closer inspection would have revealed it to be the heads and shoulders of two men, the rest of their bodies hidden from view by the grave they were digging. One of them was Eddie, the other was Delroy's cousin, Gladstone Morgan, known to his friends as Gravestone Morgue. Gladstone was six foot six inches tall, swathed in wool from head to toe – hat, scarf, mittens, leg warmers – and he was connected via headphones to an enormous 'ghetto blaster.' Every now and then, he would throw down his shovel and blow into his mittened hands. A thin, wavering strain of Rock 'n Roll would usually have been floating up on the still air into the spire of the chapel, but the batteries on Eddie's portable had given up the ghost.

'Why couldn't we use the bleedin' digger for this job,

Eddie?' said Gladstone, pushing back his headphones.

'Because, my dear gravestones,' replied Eddie, planting his shovel decisively in the earth, leaning on the handle and ignoring Gladstone's second question, 'this is going to be Mickey Gabriel's resting place, and Mickey's wife says that his last wish was to have his grave dug by hand—funny like that was Mickey.'

'Mickey Gabwiel?' said Gladstone, raising his mouth from his woollen mittens, 'who's he when he's at home cookin' jerk chicken?'

'Mickey Gabriel?' answered Eddie, 'Mickey was a Beckford boy, through and through, but he made money. He was mainly big in property, betting and used cars, but word is that he's not been averse to turning his hand to other lines of business. Word is that he got in the way of some much bigger boys who are planning some massive development down by the docks.'

'What—and they bumped him off?' said Gladstone, looking around nervously.

'Word is,' said Eddie.

'Hmmm—only Gabriel I know is an angel,' said Gladstone.

'Well, he certainly wasn't one of those, but he'll have plenty of 'em to keep him company round here,' said Eddie looking grimly around the cemetery.

'I still don't see why we couldn't have used the digger,' grumbled Gladstone.

'Maybe Mickey didn't want to feel he was being laid down like a piece of hard core under a motorway,' said Eddie, looking up into the sky as if seeking confirmation from the soul of the departed, 'though he'll probably end up that way if they build the link road through here. Anyhow, let's get on with it or we'll be 'ere all night.'

'Tcha man,' grumbled Gladstone, reluctantly picking up his shovel and replacing his headphones.

For a while, the two men worked in silence, doggedly back-to-back, or more accurately Eddie worked in silence while Gladstone worked in his exclusive world of sound. At one point, Eddie tried to make conversation at the top of his voice but got no response. He gave up and tried to concentrate on the digging, but he gradually became aware of the persistent and repetitive beat above the sound of shovelling, no more than a metallic tinkle compared to the waves of sound passing through Gladstone's head, but enough to aggravate Eddie. Now it was his turn to throw down his shovel.

'What the Fuckam's do you get out of that reggae Graves? I mean, it's all the same ain't it?'

Gladstone's back twitched slightly but other than that there was no response.

'Gordon Bennett, it's like working with a flaming zombie,' said Eddie in disgust, but even as he bent to pick up his shovel an idea began to form in his head and a broad grin spread across his face. He didn't pick up his shovel, but instead reached over the parapet and drew an armful of snow towards him, glancing at Gladstone every now and again to make sure he remained ignorant of his preparations. Then he began to knead the snow, and when he had constructed a ball roughly the size of a human head, he balanced it in one hand and with the other reached out to the volume control on Gladstone's blaster. He waited for a moment until his victim was stooped with a shovel full of earth, then flipped the control to maximum. Gladstone's reaction was as immediate and spectacular as anyone who suddenly feels that his head has been placed between nutcrackers of sound. He snapped upright, letting out a high-pitched scream which quickly descended into a bass roar as he tore off the headphones and turned to face Eddie, whereupon he received the large snowball full in the face. The roar ceased abruptly, turned into a splutter, and by the time it had become a roar again Eddie was dancing on the edge of the grave and pelting Gladstone with smaller snowballs. One mighty leap took Gladstone out of the grave and jerked the headphones out of their socket, filling the whole cemetery with a reverberating reggae beat. Eddie fled cackling across the little snowfield of the clearing and Gladstone came shambling after him, though his progress was impeded by one of his unwound scarves, which kept tripping him up and sending him flat on his face in the snow.

Puffing and blowing, Eddie finally turned with his back to the brick wall of the gothic chapel. He was so weak with laughter that he couldn't walk another step, and his bruised ribs were hurting him at every breath. Gladstone came staggering up, covered with snow and trailing his scarves behind him, like a mummy in a low budget horror film. He was carrying an armful of snow balls, and although he was trying to look menacing, he was also struggling to keep a straight face.

'One last request,' said Eddie, flinging up his arm in a theatrical gesture just as Gladstone was about to begin the execution.

'Eh?' said Gladstone.

'Before I face the firing squad,' said Eddie, producing

his tobacco with a flourish and snapping out a cigarette paper. 'Mind if I smoke?'

Eddie rolled a thin one, lit up, and stood to attention against the wall, letting out a puff or two of smoke, his working drapes steaming from his exertion, his face impassive and expressionless, the laughter in his eyes concealed by his new shades. Gladstone drew back his arm to throw, but the sight was too much for him. A chuckle started deep in his stomach and rapidly spread upwards to erupt from his mouth in such a bellow of laughter that he dropped all his snowballs and had to lean against a stone angel for support. Then, when the danger had passed, Eddie stepped forward and offered his hand to Gladstone who was now lying on the ground in a kind of seizure of laughter.

'I thought you was the one,' panted Gladstone, recovering his breath a little, 'who wanted this arse's grave dug today?'

'What, Mickey Gabriel?' said Eddie, sitting on a fallen angel and puffing on his fag, 'Yeah, let's finish him off if we can—word was that he was a bit of a hero in his way.'

'Makes no difference to me anyways,' said Gladstone, 'today's my last day—I've got a new job starting tomorrow.'

'You never told me that,' said Eddie, feeling slightly aggrieved, 'you're a dark horse, if you'll pardon the expression?'

'Yeah, sorry, Eddie, but I didn't hear until this morning, and I KNEW I would spoil your day if I told you right away. So yeah, I've got a job as a driver down at Percy Dalton's.'

'Bet that pays peanuts,' cackled Eddie, quick as a flash – (Percy Dalton's Peanut Factory was one of the most important employers in Beckford).

'Your wit, as always, is razor sharp,' said Gladstone, 'but I'm gonna miss you man, 'spite of your shit music, shit weed and shit dress sense!'

The two men shook hands and walked slowly back to the grave where the blaster was still pumping out sounds. Eddie looked down at the cold face of an angel which lay near the grave.

"Ere, Graves, give us a hand with this old fellah, will ya?' he said, as a vision appeared in his mind's eye, 'let's see if we can shift him.'

After a few minutes of cussing and puffing, they had managed to set the fallen angel up at the head of Mickey Gabriel's grave, then they completed the digging. By the time they finished, it was twilight. Eddie looked up at the other three angels which stood on columns near the grave, noticing that one had lost its cap and cloak of snow, and that there was something about its outline against the dying light which set it apart from the others. The reggae came to an end with an echoing shout which faded slowly into silence.

In the west, orange and vermilion clouds clashed violently with the turquoise sky, producing a sunset so garish that an artist would have been ridiculed for faithfully capturing it on canvas. Two airliners flashed briefly as the sun caught them, then disappeared like sky rockets. Eddie tugged at Gladstone's sleeve, 'There, that should please his missus and the family—plenty of angels to look out for him,' he said with a note of satisfaction in his voice, 'you wouldn't think he weighed that much just lookin' at him now wouldya?' he whispered.

'He looks as if he's floatin', don't he?' Gladstone replied with a slight quaver in his voice. He was right. It was now so dark that the sides and bottom of the grave had become invisible, giving it the appearance of a pool of black and oily water above which hovered the glimmering figure of the angel, relaxed, eyes closed, hands placed piously on his chest in an attitude of prayer.

'Jeezuz! This place gives me the creeps, man! I'm off,' said Gladstone, picking up his shovel and blaster.

'Yeah, okay Graves—I hope Percy is good to you,' said Eddie, holding out his hand, 'but before you go, I've got a little surprise for you of my own—me and Reen are getting married. We'd like it a lot if you can come to the wedding.'

'Wow man — 'who's a dark horse now then?' said Gladstone smiling broadly, 'I'd be honoured. See you both there if not before,' he said, slapping Eddie's palm before loping off across the snow towards the cemetery gate, trailing a scarf behind him.

Chapter 7

Let's Get Together

Eddie watched until Gladstone had disappeared into the gloom, then he bent down and picked up his own shovel, bag of smaller tools and dead cassette player before turning to go. On the edge of the clearing he stopped, took a last glance around him to make sure he hadn't left anything behind, and noticed at once that the familiar scene had changed slightly. Something was missing, though he couldn't immediately work out what it was. He scratched his head and lowered his shades, which gave him a brighter but hazier view of the scene and began to roll a fag.

Then all at once he stiffened, his tongue sticking out in the very act of licking the paper. For he had just realised what was missing. There were no longer three angels looking down on Mickey Gabriel's grave—one stone column was vacant. The realisation had hardly begun to sink in before an icy wind sprang up from nowhere, whipping the feathery snow from the bare bones of the trees. A moment later, Eddie once again heard the sound which had scared the daylights out of him down by the Limehouse Basin, and at the same time he saw a shadow rushing towards him across the white floor of the clearing, a shadow like the one a small cloud might cast on a field of corn on a bright, blowing summer's day. Then, as he dived full length onto the snow, he had a momentary vision of a formation of stony-faced, pin-striped city gents, rhythmically opening and closing their black umbrellas in some kind of nightmarish Busby Berkeley routine.

'FU-DGERIGAR!'

When Eddie started feeling that his nose would fall off if he lay where he was a second longer, he gingerly raised his face from the snow and looked about him. The wind had dropped, and the clearing was still. He timidly looked up into the sky, but the heavens were once again quite empty except for a few early stars. Then he turned to look at the three columns overlooking Mickey's grave, and when he saw that they were all occupied once more he got to his feet and ran for the gates as he had never run in his life before. It was then that he heard a voice, above the tortuous sound of his own breathing and the thundering of his heart. It was a rich, rather aristocratic voice that formed a single word, which reached him across the cemetery.

'NINCOMPOOP!'

Now he could see the gates, about a hundred yards away at the end of a long avenue of trees, and beyond them a street lamp had come on which, for a moment, seemed to Eddie like a beacon guiding him to safety. Wrong! Before he had run more than a few strides, a group of figures, silhouetted by the light, strode through the gates and stood in a line across the avenue, blocking his path. Eddie's heart sank. He didn't need more than a silhouette to know who they were.

'Oi, Baldecott, workin' late, are we? You should know it ain't good for your 'ealth to be workin' after dark. You should be tucked up with your hot chocolate by now.'

Eddie recognised the speaker at once. It was Goliath. For a moment, he experienced a feeling of panic and despair—Gladstone was long gone and no one else was likely to come into the cemetery now. In front of him were six skins aching for revenge, and behind him...?

'Fuck me—sorry 'Reen!' muttered Eddie to himself, taking a firm grip on his shovel and pulling out a hammer before throwing the tool bag into the bushes and turning on his heel to run.

Luckily for Eddie at least three of the skinheads, including the leader, were no fitter than him, so that the two youngest and fittest—and stupidest—were the first to reach the clearing, ignoring their leader's orders to 'Stay together, you fuckin' twats.' By that time Eddie had positioned himself directly behind Mickey Gabriel's open grave, which was now completely invisible in the darkness, and flicked open the Zippo to show them where he was standing.

'Come on then, you grapefruits, whatcha waitin' for?'

The two young skins, eager for glory, ran full tilt at Eddie and promptly disappeared into the deep grave, knocking their heads together as they fell. Before they had time to get up, Eddie had put his shoulder behind the stone angel which obligingly toppled over and into the grave, pinning them both down long enough for Eddie to whack each of them on the head with his shovel before running to the door of the chapel which he kicked open with two or three hefty blows from his working crepes. At least there the skins could only come at him one at a time.

Inside it was pitch black until he took off his shades. Even then the light from the small, cobwebbed windows was only enough to give him a dim idea of his surroundings. The

83

floor of the chapel seemed completely empty, though a darker patch at the far end of the little room suggested that there might be an opening there, maybe a hatch leading to a lower room or cellar—which would be even better for defending himself. There was also a strange smell in the room, a smell that was somehow familiar. He stole a blurry glance out into the clearing and could just make out the third skinhead running up to the grave in which the two young ones lay groaning.

'What the fuck!' he said looking around the clearing. Eddie took a step or two back from the door and as he did, so his right crepe caught on something which sent him sprawling full length amongst a cacophony of falling tin cans in the clattering darkness.

'BLEEDIN' BLOATED BUDGIES,' cried Eddie, groping on the floor for his dropped shades at the same time as hearing the third skin calling out to the others:

'Oi lads, 'e's in the building, whatever it is, I'll 'ave 'im!'

Then another voice, much, much closer:

'NINCOMPOOP'

Eddie, on all fours, stopped dead, unsure whether his ears had deceived him in the racket of falling cans. Then the voice came again, even closer now, and it was the same rich, aristocratic voice that he had heard before – quiet, calm irritation expressed in measured tones.

'How very tiresome of you to ruin my burglar alarm, Eddie—have you any conception of how long it takes me to construct one of those things?'

"E's in 'ere lads,' came the voice of the third skinhead. As Eddie shuffled round on the floor, he could just see the skin's blurred silhouette against the dim light from the doorway. He was raising his arm above his head holding the hammer which Eddie had dropped after clouting the young skins with his shovel.

'Say your prayers, Teddy Boy!'

Eddie thought of Maureen and the twins at the same time as the sweet sickly smell filled his nostrils. It reminded him of the aroma which Ron and Derek produced after too many baked beans, but it was ten times more pungent.

Then came a wicked hissing noise and for a fraction of a second another silhouette appeared like a great falling scythe that seemed to brush the figure in the doorway with the sound of a green banana being peeled, followed by the loud breaking of wind. There was a scream of pain, the clatter of Eddie's hammer on the chapel floor, receding bovver boots and a voice squealing and echoing in the clearing outside.

'Oh no, oh no, oh shh… oh nooooooooooo—my fuckin' ear, oh Christ— 'e's cut off me fuckin' ear!'

Eddie remained mesmerised in the same position for a few moments, open-mouthed and gawping, until a calm voice came out of the darkness behind him, and he felt the shades being pushed back onto his nose.

Eddie leaped up and took a few steps backwards, stumbling on the baked bean cans again.

'Dear, dear Eddie, you really must try to be more careful,' came the voice, followed by the sound of metal scraping on stone, 'they'll be back in a minute, dear boy, and you don't want to be tangling with your pal Goliath again, do you? I wouldn't like to be in your crepes when they catch up with you, so you'd better follow me.'

Eddie opened his mouth to speak, but no words came.

The voice from the darkness supplied the question.

'Who am I? It's a long story dear boy, and there's no time to go into it now—are you coming or not?'

Eddie fumbled in his drape for the Zippo, held it above his head, and struck the flint with a shaking hand. What he saw by the flickering flame almost made him drop the lighter: a few feet away, in the act of descending into an open manhole, was a creature of nightmare. Its head was quite bald and set with two bright red, lidless eyes on either side of a long, pale, pelican-like beak, the tip of which was still dripping with the skinhead's blood. A goitrous appendage of wrinkled skin hung down beneath its lower jaw and was attached to its thick, scaly neck just above a prominent Adam's apple. The lower part of its body was invisible, but it seemed to be wearing a kind of leather cloak wrapped around its shoulders. What looked like a reddish, pointed cap stuck out, almost jauntily, from the back of its skull. The creature opened its beak.

'Sorry, Eddie, forgot you people can't see in the dark.' Two translucent membranes flicked across the glowing eyes. Then its head turned at the sound of shouting and the thunder of approaching bovver boots out in the clearing. 'I think I hear the patter of tiny feet—it's time we were on our way dear boy.'

At last Eddie found his voice. 'But you're... you're a bleedin'...bird!'

The creature breathed a tolerant sigh. 'No, I'm not a 'bleedin' bird' as you so crudely put it.'

'An angel then...'

'No, not an angel either. If you must know, I'm a Pteranodon—though you people sometimes mistakenly call me a Pterodactyl, when in fact they're from a quite different branch of the family. They're from the Lower Jurassic, you see, while we're from the Upper Cretaceous,' said the creature with more than a hint of snobbery in its voice. 'Anyway, this is not the time or place for a natural history lesson. I'm off. You can stay and face the music if you like.'

Eddie looked out of the doorway and saw that Goliath and the others were halfway across the clearing but approaching warily following the damage already inflicted on three of them. Then he looked back at the manhole. The creature had disappeared and was drawing the cover into place from below.

'Wait!' shouted Eddie and scrambled to the edge of the manhole. The cover slid back a little.

'All right old chap,' came the voice from the darkness, 'but make sure you pull the cover tight behind you and bolt it from underneath.'

Eddie lowered himself into the hole, felt for the rungs of the metal ladder beneath him and pulled the cover over his head and into place. Then, when he had shot the bolts home on the underside, he extinguished the Zippo and gingerly began to descend.

'Christ! came a pained voice from below him, 'Mind where you're putting your dirty great plates of meat, will you?'

'Sorry, chief,' muttered Eddie, apologetically.

It was probably just as well that the darkness in the shaft was total, otherwise Eddie might have been tempted to look down. As it was, he wasn't so terrified that he couldn't move, but he was terrified enough that he was unable to take one hand off the ladder to relight the Zippo. He climbed down what seemed like about a hundred cold, iron rungs, then stopped and looked up, straining his lids apart as if his eyes might suddenly open and he would be looking at the bedroom ceiling with Maureen by his side. Instead, tiny specks of light began to fizz before his eyes, like a TV screen left on after 'closedown.'

'Oi, chief,' said Eddie, unable to keep the quaver out of his voice, 'How much further is it?'

A horribly distant reply floated up from down below,

'Not far now dear boy.'

'How far is not far?' shouted Eddie. A few moments passed, then an even fainter voice answered.

'Come along man, we haven't got all day—I'll catch you if you fall.'

The thought of being caught by the creature increased Eddie's determination to hang on to the ladder at all costs, and he began his slow descent once more. As he did so, the specks of light in front of his eyes began to fall like hail, which soon turned into thick blobs of snow. Eddie was almost considering taking the creature up on its offer when his left crepe finally struck bottom.

He remained motionless, unable to trust his own sensations, then carefully lowered his right foot. That touched bottom too. He took two or three deep breaths, then pulled out the Zippo, struck the flint, then jumped back onto the ladder in fright. The creature was leaning against a wall not four feet away, its leathery cape wrapped around its body, one clawed foot crossed over the other. It was looking at Eddie with a tolerant, slightly amused expression.

'Spose, you think that's funny?' said Eddie when he had recovered his composure a little and got back down off the ladder. The creature uncrossed its legs and wrinkled its raisin-skin brow.

'Sorry, dear boy, I'm not quite with you there?'

'Makin' me go through that bleedin' performance. I could have fallen to my death.'

'Oh come, come, Eddie,' said the creature with a slightly disdainful shrug. 'Would you rather have faced your friends up there? I'm sure the 'earless wonder' would have found you hard to forgive, never mind the two babes in the grave—oh, and Goliath, of course! Anyway, nobody forced you to come with me, did they?'

'All right then—you've got a point, chief. I really should thank you, but what do we do now?'

'Do?' said the creature, 'well, you can begin by thanking me, then we do nothing for an hour or so, then you pop back up to see if the coast is clear. I wouldn't waste your fuel if I were you, old chap. You'll need some light to find the bolts on the underside of the cover,'

'Pop?' said Eddie, 'Pop? Look chief, if you were a dozen grapefruits instead of a... er...whatever you are, I'd rather stay and fight here than 'pop' back up that bleedin' ladder.'

As Eddie spoke, the flame of the Zippo flickered and grew dimmer.

'Come on chief, there must be another way out.'

The creature tugged reflectively at its goitre with its clawed digits.

'Well, yes, there is actually, but it's a long way round and will involve a little...'

'I don't care what it involves so long as I don't have to climb no ladders,' said Eddie.

'No ladders,' said the creature.

'Right, lead on then squire,' said Eddie. 'Oi, half a mo', how d'you know my name anyway?'

'Oh, I've been watching you for some time, Eddie,' said the creature, setting off down a narrow passageway which led out of the little chamber at the bottom of the ladder. 'Believe me, you're hard to miss,' it said, over its shoulder. 'By the way, you can call me Pterry if you like?'

'Bleedin' cheek!' muttered Eddie as he followed Pterry into the darkness.

Chapter 8

Latch On

Eddie stumbled along behind his saviour, the pitch darkness only barely kept at bay by the flickering light of the Zippo. Very slowly he became aware of another sound above the swishing of Pterry's 'cloak' and the squishing of his own crepe boppers. It was a deep, roaring sound, very faint at first but gradually growing in volume, and with it came a smell which was quite different from Pterry's pungent body odour. At last, they stopped before a great metal door which blocked their path.

'Give me a hand with this will you, old chap?' said Pterry, bending over the wheel which was set in the middle of the door. 'Sometimes it's a bit stiff.'

Eddie hesitated for a moment, then extinguished the Zippo and felt for the rim of the wheel in the pitch blackness. His hands closed over something cold, hard and tubular and he began to twist it to the left.

'Ouch! That's my wing finger you great nitwit,' came Pterry's pained voice. Eddie fumbled for the Zippo.

'Sorry... er... Mr Terror.'

'No come on, you don't need the lighter.' said Pterry, 'Here.' Something which felt like a large pair of pliers grasped Eddie's wrist and guided his hand to the rim of the wheel.

'Got it?'

'Yup,' said Eddie

'Right, on the count of three then—one, two, three and…'

Eddie and Pterry strained downwards with all their might, but the wheel didn't budge.

'Once more then, one, two three and…' again they grunted and strained in vain.

'My oath, she's a bit stubborn today, though I must confess I haven't used this route for a month or two,' said Pterry. 'It could probably do with a drop of Three-in-One—you don't happen to have a can on you do you Eddie?'

'Oh bother,' said Eddie in a mock posh voice, 'I seem to have left mine at home this morning, your lordship. Bleedin' marvellous, ain't it?'

'Sarcasm really doesn't become you, does it?' said Pterry drily. Then Eddie had a brain wave.

'Half a mo', though,' he said, a note of real excitement in his voice, 'this might do the trick.' Eddie lit the Zippo and put it down carefully on the stone floor beneath the wheel. Then he produced a tube of Tru-gel hair cream from his drape and began to squirt the clear grease into the crevice between the wheel hub and the main door—and into any other aperture or cranny he could find. When he had emptied what was left in the tube, he wiped his hands on his handkerchief, spat on them, rubbed them together and took a firm grip on the wheel.

'You ready then, Mr Terror?'

'Certainly,' said Pterry, 'though I really cannot see how you can bring yourself to put that stuff on your hair.'

"Course, you'd know all about hair, wouldn'tcha, Mr Terror?' said Eddie. 'On the count of three—a-one-a, a-two-a, a-three-a and...' Nothing, except a loud fart from Pterry.

''Scuse you Mr Terror! Once again then, one, two, three and...' this time there was a shriek of metal on metal from deep in the door.

'By Jove—I think you might have cracked it dear boy!' said Pterry.

The Zippo went out with a little pop.

'All right, it's now or never,' grunted Eddie into the darkness, in which only Pterry's burning red eyes were now visible. 'Let's give it all we've got this time—one, two three and...' The wheel gave almost immediately, sending them both sprawling on the floor.

Hooting with triumph, Eddie got to his feet, this time pulling rather than twisting the wheel. But as the door swung open his celebration was stifled by a mighty roar of sound and a wave of the most nauseating air he had ever breathed. He staggered forward a few paces before Pterry caught his arm and shouted in his ear.

'Steady on old man, you'll come a nasty cropper if you go any further in that direction. You'll get used to the smell in a few minutes—oh, and here's your lighter,' he said, slipping the Zippo into Eddie's hand, 'but whatever you do, PLEASE don't try to strike it!

Eddie was so dazed he didn't register what Pterry was saying and instinctively flipped back the cap of the Zippo then rolled his finger along the little wheel.

'Eddie, no!' shouted Pterry, but it was too late.

The shower of little white sparks was immediately followed by a sound like a massive gas oven igniting. Two tongues of bluish flame unrolled from Eddie's hand like ectoplasm, hovered above him for a moment as if uncertain where to go, then blossomed into countless tendrils of delicate fire which illuminated their surroundings with a strange and ethereal light. They were standing on a small platform let into the wall of an enormous tunnel. Below Eddie—and for as far as he could see to right and left—the will o' the wisp which he had just set free was dancing and flickering across the black surface of the roaring, echoing torrent which thundered through the tunnel a few yards below their feet.

'Welcome to Bazalgette's Northern Outfall,' Pterry said, above the din.

'Eh, wassat?' asked Eddie, still open-mouthed with amazement.

'Sewage and methane, old man—the sort of stuff that flowed through the streets of London and filled the Thames before Mr B. had this bright idea—you've just set fire to the fart gas of the entire population of London north of the Thames!'

Eddie still didn't seem to hear what Pterry was saying. He remained standing with his hand raised above his head, staring down as if hypnotised by the scene he had created. The Zippo fell from his hand into the torrent, but still, he didn't move. It was only when he heard the sound of huge umbrellas opening in the dark, unmistakeable even against the Outfall's uproar, that he regained his faculties to some extent and looked behind him. What he saw would probably have made him fall off the platform and join the Zippo in the black, swirling sewage below had he not still been in a state of semi-hypnosis. Pterry had removed his leather 'cloak'—or to be more accurate, he had transformed the cloak into a pair of enormous wings which he was busy stretching and carefully examining.

'This is where we stop acting like moles, dear boy. Ready to fly, are you?' said Pterry, waddling rather awkwardly to the parapet and spreading his magnificent wings to their full extent. 'Hop on—it's not far, really.'

'Fly?' said Eddie in a hollow, distant voice. The suggestion was so fantastical, so outrageous even by comparison with what he had already endured, that he could do nothing but acquiesce. And to be fair, there was no alternative. 'Hop on,' he whispered, 'yeah, hop on why don't I?' He walked round behind Pterry to assess the chances of climbing onto his back.

For a while, Eddie's arms and legs worked mechanically at the task like a clockwork toy which encounters an obstruction while crossing the nursery floor. He had never been the nimblest of men and he was still dazed, so he just couldn't get any purchase on Pterry's scaly skin.

'Hang onto my comb and I'll pull you up,' said Pterry, tilting his neck so that the osseous protrusion on the back of his head came within Eddie's reach.

'Eh?' said Eddie, 'Comb?' thinking vaguely about the oily quiff-manipulator in the back pocket of his drains.

'Oh Eddie, do get a grip on yourself, my comb, the thing on the back of my head—my hat, if you like. It's quite solid, it won't come off,' Pterry continued, tilting his head and neck even further back. 'What's the matter with you? You must be able to reach it now? Once you're on my back, let go of the comb and take a grip round my neck—but don't let go, whatever you do, or you'll be in the drink.'

Slowly Eddie raised his hands, grasped Pterry's comb firmly and then...

'Allez-oop!'

Pterry straightened his powerful neck, lifting Eddie off his feet, and projected himself and his passenger into the abyss, breaking wind loudly at the same time. Luckily, the experience had shocked Eddie out of his trance, but even so he almost slid off into the Outfall.

'Good lord you're heavy, hold on tight!' said Pterry who had plummeted dangerously close to the surface of the sewage before starting to gain height with some prodigious wingbeats.

This time Eddie obeyed orders at once and hung on for dear life. 'Billions of blue bonneted budgerigars!' he hissed between clenched teeth, his hands just meeting around Pterry's bulging neck.

'Careful of my Adam's apple,' spluttered Pterry, as Eddie felt something hard moving up and down beneath the leathery skin like a kitten under a blanket. He wasn't going to change or relax his grip for love nor money. In fact, he was almost beginning to wish he was back on the ladder.

The ride was short, but terrifying—about ten times more so than his Bank Holiday Monday rides on the Wild Mouse at the Kursaal fun fair in Southend. But by the end of it, Eddie's terror had crossed that indefinable barrier and turned into sheer exhilaration. In places Pterry's wing tips all but brushed the sides of the tunnel, and now and again he had to rake them back to avoid a protruding platform or negotiate a sudden chicane.

'Could have been a bit tricky if Mr B. had built this tunnel any narrower!' shouted Pterry. 'Keep an eye open for

great big floating lumps of fat, hair and God knows what—
we may need to take a different route if we come across one
of them. They're becoming a real problem in the Outfall—
people up above just don't know what they are creating down
here when they chuck stuff down the drains.'

Eddie nodded vigorously in agreement, not having the
faintest idea of what one of these might look like. From his
position, squinting grimly over Pterry's right shoulder, it
seemed as if he was astride a sharp-snouted shell, rushing
down the barrel of some enormous gun, the entire length of
which was filled with the flame of cordite that was the will o'
the wisp, constantly mutating like organisms beneath a
microscope, here gathering into great balls of fire, there
stretching into the finest filigree of light.

After about a minute's flying time, the journey ended as
abruptly and terrifyingly as it had begun. With twenty or
thirty rapid wingbeats, Pterry accelerated to his maximum
airspeed, then went into a steep climb. At the last moment,
and with a shout of 'Hang on tight!' he folded his wings and
shot into a black hole in the roof of the tunnel. Eddie closed
his eyes tight and hung on for grim death, not letting go until
he dimly heard Pterry's choking voice pleading with him to
do so. Even then it took him several seconds to reassure
himself that he was on solid ground, to relinquish his grip
and to slide from Pterry's back into a sitting position, still
keeping his eyes tight shut.

'Good God man, I thought you were never going to let
go!'

At the sound of that plummy voice, Eddie convinced
himself that he really was awake, opened his eyes and looked
around. Pterry was massaging his goitre and was perched like

a grotesque budgerigar on a trapeze which hung a few feet from the floor of the oddest room Eddie had ever seen. It was circular, and bare except for a pile of twenty or thirty neatly stacked cardboard boxes. It was lit only by a series of very small, very dirty windows which started at floor level and spiralled upwards, letting in the yellow glow of neon from outside. In the dim light, the walls seemed at first to have been constructed from bricks of irregular shapes and sizes, laid vertically rather than horizontally. However, on closer inspection the 'bricks' turned out to be books, ring upon ring of them, running around the entire circumference of the room and reaching up through the darkness towards a sixpenny-sized disc of starlight far above Eddie's head.

'Am I dead or what?' croaked Eddie, getting slowly to his feet, 'Is this heaven?'

'No Eddie, your time has not yet come,' said Pterry in his most condescending, superior tone of voice, 'though not for want of trying.'

'God almighty, where are we then? And what's this...this gaff?' asked Eddie, head back, gazing upwards in awe before his mind wandered to a more down to earth request.

''Scuse me Mr Terror, have you got a light on you?'

Pterry, swinging gently on his trapeze, answered the question with a look of such withering disdain that Eddie rapidly returned his tobacco and Rizlas to his drape pocket.

'Don't be alarmed Eddie, you're not far from home and you can indulge in whatever DISGUSTING habits you like as soon as you get back. This 'gaff'—as you so quaintly put it—is one of the only two remaining examples of Bazalgette's Patent Smoke Conducting and Filtering

Chimney, and it is situated at the Beckford end of the Northern Outfall Sewer.'

'A chimbly? This? Crikey, I know exactly where we are then! I walk past your gaff two or three times a week—who'd have thought you were peering out at me!' said Eddie with a smile which rapidly vanished from his face. 'Oh Jeeezuz,' he groaned, putting his hands to his head, 'Maureen—what about Reenie—I've got to see her Mr Terry!'

'Don't worry, Eddie, all in good time,' said Pterry, 'I know it seems like hours, but our journey has taken less time than a walk to the Samson from the Mansions. I also know how much you care for Maureen and the twins, for your mum and dad and for all your friends—and for Beckford—and I know about the plans you're hatching to make them all happy. The problem is you're a GREAT LUMMOX, dear boy.'

'Eh? You what?' said Eddie, baffled by how Pterry had come to know so much about him. He was uncertain whether to glow with pride or erupt in rage. Instead, he sat down on one of the cardboard boxes and leaned forward with his head in his hands, trying to take in what was happening to him. Between his legs he read the words 'Crosse and Blackwell Baked Beans' printed on the box.

'Blimey, is this all you eat, Mr Terry?' said Eddie, remembering the familiar sounds and smells.

'That and the occasional pug, poodle or pussy cat if I'm desperate—and maybe a skinhead's ear now and then,' said Pterry, swinging gently on the trapeze and eyeing Eddie intently.

'Well don't eat Papworth or I'll kill you!' said Eddie, a smile returning briefly to his face, before disappearing again.

'Let's face it, Eddie, said Pterry, gliding down from his perch and sitting beside the forlorn Teddy Boy, 'neither of us is getting any younger and we can't do what we used to do on our own—so maybe working together will be a solution?'

'Maybe you're right, Mr Terry,' said Eddie, standing up, his hands on his hips, 'but I've no idea how that might work, to be honest. All I know is that I'm comin' up to my life's half way house and I'm earning Jack Shit—how can I look after my family, let alone any possible new additions. I keep on gettin' aggravation from the grapefruits—and I didn't get a penny in sick pay after the last working over they gave me! What I really need is money!'

'Ah! 'Don't we all? But it's the terms under which we acquire it that must be examined. It's a popular romantic misconception in this society that an individual can maintain his or her self-respect without having money. Poverty can corrupt just as surely as power and wealth. Of course, the point at which one becomes corrupted by money—or the lack of it—depends on the individual. Even in this society there are those at the top and the bottom of the pile who remain uncorrupted, but they are very few.'

Pterry paused to draw breath in the middle of his peroration but seeing Eddie looking mystified he shuffled closer to him.

'Now then, Eddie,' he began again in a confidential tone, 'I'm going to let you into a secret. You may think that because I am—well, what I am—and because I pursue, shall we say, a rather unconventional lifestyle—that it means I don't need money. But you'd be wrong! In fact, my life is being threatened at this very moment because I have no money.' Pterry paused again and looked wistfully up towards the disc of light. There was more than a hint of tearfulness in his voice when he resumed.

'Look around you. This old chimney—one of my two remaining homes—will be pulled down before the end of the year. It will be pulled down by people who have got lots of money—but want more. In its place, they are going to build a block of flats overlooking the canal where people with lots of money can live. In the old days, there were lots of buildings like this where Pteranodons like me could live, but now they are few and far between—and it's not just Pteranodons who are feeling the squeeze. My friend Leslie, the Plesiosaur, who migrates in summer from the Limehouse Basin to Loch Ness, is facing the same problem. You might have seen him on one of your walks along the canal? Word is the same people who bumped off Mickey Gabriel are going to build a massive tower where the Basin is now—so Leslie will have nowhere to migrate to once he has finished his summer spreading rumours and entertaining the tourists north of the border!'

'Oh yeah, I thought something odd was goin' on down there the other day,' said Eddie, 'does he eat the occasional guard dog and eel fisherman when he gets hungry?'

'Quite possibly,' said Pterry with a smile, 'but who can blame him? That kind of tasty snack is getting harder to come by up in Loch Ness with the salmon in decline and every Tom, Dick and Harry on the lookout with a pair of binoculars or some sort of sonar device! It's also a very long swim up the North Sea to Inverness and, via a series of canals and rivers, to Loch Ness. As you say, neither of us are getting any younger, and moving house isn't that easy any more,' he continued, looking up at his myriad books. 'And of course, there's my poor little Towser the Triceratops to feed—here boy!' Out from the shadows ambled a creature about the size of a large, stocky Labrador but with a parrot-like beak and three horns on its head, one above each eye and a smaller one on the end of its beak. At the back of its head, a kind of bony ruff spread out, like a giant flea collar in reverse.

'Blimey—and I thought I'd seen it all,' muttered Eddie.

'His parents were killed when they demolished the old biscuit factory in Poplar and were laying foundations for a new motorway flyover—they wandered into a pit of liquid concrete and sank without trace. Just like the old tar pits, I suppose. They'll be scratching their heads if they ever dig them up,' said Pterry, thoughtfully stroking Towser behind his ruff and giving him a large carrot to crunch. 'Oh, I need money all right dear boy, and I won't pretend that I haven't been tempted to employ some unorthodox methods of getting hold of it—being able to fly does have its advantages in the burglary game. I can almost see the headlines now: 'Batman Bullion Snatch' or maybe 'Hang-Glider Heist'!'

Pterry gazed pensively into space and tugged at his goitre, a half-smile momentarily lighting up his face before leathery folds began to gather again on his brow.

'No, I can no more make that much money than you can, Eddie, not without selling my soul to the devil, that is.'

'Seems like we've both had it then, Mr T,' said Eddie.

'On our own, I fear you would be right my boy, but collectively we may still have a chance to help each other out of this spot.'

'Eh?'

'United we stand and all that.'

'What you on about, Mr T?'

Pterry leaned forward until the tip of his beak was almost

touching Eddie's nose. 'The first thing you must realise,' he said with a soft but urgent tone to his voice, 'is that the people who are coming to pull down my chimney are not going to stop there. Within a year, sooner if they can make it, they are going to widen Beckford High Street and demolish the Samson and The Happy Sole to make a motorway to the Isle of Dogs. Next, Paragon Road and The Bloody Mary will be gone to make room for a link road to the motorway, and at the same time, they will relocate Beckford cemetery and build a multiple flyover to join the two projects.'

'Relocate?' whispered Eddie in a daze, 'but what they goin' to do with all the stiffs?'

'Dig 'em up, dear boy—those they can find, that is—and re-plant them elsewhere. They won't be too fussed trying to match up the gravestones, though.'

'Where?' asked Eddie

'Where what?'

'Where they goin' to... relocate it?'

'Penge.'

'Penge. They can't bleedin' well do that!' said Eddie, his voice suddenly rising.

'They say there's nowhere nearer to put them.'

'But half my bleedin' family's buried there—more than half. What would great uncle Toby say if he knew they were takin' him sarf of the river? Most of them would prefer to be concreted over rather than move down there.' Eddie paused for a moment, then shook his head. 'Nah, they wouldn't do that, not in a million years. How do I know all this is really goin' to happen anyway, Mr Terror?'

Pterry didn't answer. Instead, he returned to his trapeze and pulled on a rope which propelled him upwards into the gloom. Within a few minutes, he returned with a small cassette tape recorder, similar to Eddie's portable. He placed it on the baked bean box next to Eddie and pressed 'play.'

Two men were talking. One had a posh English voice, not unlike Pterry's. The other spoke with a thick southern American drawl. They were talking about their plans for the area, saying more or less everything Pterry had just been saying.

'Heard enough?' asked Pterry, pressing the 'stop' button with a bony digit.

'Who are those two, for Chrissake?' shouted Eddie, jumping to his feet.

'You don't need to know just now,' replied Pterry quietly, 'in fact, I think it's probably better that you know as little as possible for the moment. Suffice it to say that THEY are your real enemies—not the rockabillies. Not even Goliath and his grapefruits!'

'But they can't bleedin' well do all those things they were talkin' about? Can they?'

'Oh yes, they can. Provided you've got a bit of paper signed by someone in authority, you can do just about anything to anyone in this poor old country of ours. But...' here Pterry paused, and his ruby eyes flashed, 'if it can be proved that you got that piece of paper through bribery and corruption, THEN YOU ARE IN TROUBLE! That's what I and my friends have been working on, and I think I'm getting near to putting together a good enough case.'

'Good enough case? You ought to go to the law right away Mr T.'

'Oh yes, Eddie, and who do you think would trust a penniless Pterandodon? No one would believe their eyes, let alone their ears.'

'Well, I'll do it then,' said Eddie forcefully, standing up and waving his hands in the air.

'Oh come, come Eddie. People would only be marginally more likely to believe you than they would me. No, we've got to make people know who we are. We've got to become rich and famous—or just famous, to start with at least. Then people will sit up and take notice.'

'And just how do you propose to do that, eh?' asked Eddie.

Pterry tugged pensively at his goitre, then pulled hard on the rope next to his trapeze and shot up into the darkness again, this time returning with a magazine clutched in his digit.

'There may just be a way, but as I said, we're going to have to face the world together. Ever been on TV, dear boy?' he said tossing the magazine into Eddie's lap. 'This might give you an idea of how we might find fame and fortune together.' The magazine was open at a full-page colour spread of Michael Parkinson being attacked by Rod Hull's Emu on Parky's chat show.'

'Yeah, I remember seein' that in the papers,' said Eddie, 'but how's this goin' to help us?'

'Oh come, come—use your imagination. You wouldn't even have to learn to be a ventriloquist!'

'A what?'

'Dear Lord, give me strength,' sighed Pterry, 'there's a new series of that loathsome talent show *Stargazers* starting on the box in April, Eddie—and WE are going to WIN it dear boy! Are you beginning to get the picture?'

'Eh? Ohhhhhhhhhhhhhhh,' breathed Eddie, the penny

finally dropping, 'so you're goin' to be the new Emu?'

'Yeeeessss, Eddie—the light has dawned! Only I don't propose to be dumb, unlike my very, very distant antipodean cousin.'

'Eh—you've lost me again.'

'Emu never said a word, but I…I intend to sing like a canary, especially about what's proposed for our beloved Beckford!'

'And where do I fit in?'

'You? All you have to do is sit there in your Teddy Boy finest, pretending that you've got your hand up my… Well, my nether regions… and that every word I say is in fact coming from you. You will be hailed as the finest ventriloquist of the age, we will earn loads of money, preserve both of our dinosaur ways of life and everything that goes with them—and shine a light on the Beckford development racket at the same time.'

'What could be simpler?'

Eddie's mouth was hanging open in undiluted, slack-jawed amazement, but somewhere deep down in his soul a small light had come on which hadn't been there before.

'Anyway, it's high time you got back to that lovely lady of yours—this is where I must bid you a fond farewell, go out through the door and you'll soon get your bearings—it's only about ten minutes' walk to your… gaff.'

'But Mr Terror…' said Eddie, desperate for more information.

'Pterry is the name, Eddie – spelled P T E R R Y.'

'P?' queried Eddie.

'Yes, as in Ptolemy,' said Pterry with a supercilious smile. 'Oh, and Eddie, do try to stay out of trouble—if

Goliath gets hold of you it may scupper all our hopes. I'll be back in touch with you as soon as I think we can move a bit further. Meanwhile, enjoy your family, enjoy your wedding, enjoy all the things you have reason to thank the Almighty for!' He pulled on the rope and shot high up above Eddie, calling down: 'Now I've got some work to do if our plan is to bear fruit.'

'Plan?' said Eddie, scratching his head 'but when are we going to talk again?'

'Oh, I'll be around—as I said, it's a question of "don't call us, we'll call you" at least for the time being. In the meantime, only call on me as a last resort. Byeeee!'

'Wait Mr P-TERRY,' said Eddie pronouncing the P, but Pterry had hauled himself right up to the top of the chimney.

'Charmin',' said Eddie, opening the door and emerging blinking into the Beckford night. He was standing on the grassy embankment which carried the great pipes of the Northern Outfall straight as a Roman road to the distant Sewage Metropolis at Beckton. The Mansions was only a few minutes' walk from there, and as he scrambled down the bank, he thought he heard that familiar voice, now distant as if he was talking from the top of the chimney: 'The P is silent, dear boy...' He smiled, then looked up and read the brand-new notice which had been erected immediately below the chimney:

'Lea Valley Authority. Demolition Order. Northern Outfall Sewer Embankment Regeneration and Landscape Planting Scheme—Phase 1.'

'Bleedin' cheek,' thought Eddie as he felt in the pocket of his drape for his spare Zippo—he always carried two in case of emergencies. On the way home, he rolled a thin one, remembering with some amazement that he hadn't smoked since before the afternoon's adventures had begun. Maureen and the twins were fast asleep by the time he got back to the Mansions, but there was some dinner in the oven, which was still edible. After eating, Eddie peeled off his drapes, crepes and drains, put on his flannelette jim-jams, forgot to take off his shades and wriggled as quietly as he could into bed.

Chapter 9

Hallelujah, I Love her So

The miraculous April sunshine invested the landscape of Uncle Bruno's yard with a significance it did not normally possess. In the clear light, in the heat without haze, the piles of worn tyres and rusting exhaust pipes, the empty oil drums, and even the long-dry petrol pumps seemed to take on a new meaning to their existence. In January they had been inscrutable in their disguises of snow. In August, their outlines would be blurred by haze and dust. But on this April day, they were triumphantly themselves, the more so as there was not a living or moving thing in the yard to detract from their splendour.

The yard itself was also exultant in this light, proudly exhibiting its precious contents like a rectangular, glass-topped display cabinet. A double gate of peeling, painted wood and two walls of crumbling brick made up three sides of the yard. As tawdry and squalid as the things they looked down upon, they also appeared to be suggesting that all wasn't quite as it seemed.

The fourth side of the yard was formed by railway arches, seven symmetrical black caves, with their depths impervious to light, threatening to disgorge something utterly unbelievable at any moment.

The yard was filled with the particular strain of melancholy loneliness which was peculiar to such places on Sunday afternoons in East London. It was a loneliness which surpassed even that of the open sea, the snow field or the desert waste—but it was also a loneliness which had its tongue in its cheek, and which knew that the illusion it had created might vanish as soon as a cloud passed across the sun.

Within a year or two, the yard would almost certainly have disappeared beneath the motorway link road, but in the meantime, it would go on existing, like a single cell in a huge termite mound, unaware of the scale of forces operating outside the mound's seemingly invulnerable maze of passageways.

But what of the termites themselves? Nothing moved for an hour while the sun passed overhead, and the brick walls kept whispering to the wooden gates, but no termite appeared, unless you include the few pigeons which flew overhead. But then, as the chimes of St. Mary's, Beckford sounded four o'clock, a train rumbled drowsily across the arches on its meandering way down to Bow. It carried only a handful of passengers, all of them asleep except for the two Smooves who had gawped at Eddie in The Bloody Mary back in November. They were leaning out of a window and, as they passed above the yard, one of them shouted something and pointed excitedly. His words were drowned in the clanking din, but before the last coach disappeared around a curve in the line, a fat black and white tom cat, which had been disturbed by the train, emerged from its warm sleepy-hole to stretch ecstatically on top of one of the walls, forepaws extended, claws spread wide, seeming to click every joint in his spine as his fluffy, jodhpur hind legs thrust a rigid, quivering tail into the air. Satisfied, he sat back on his haunches, curled his tail neatly around his paws, unhinged his jaws and yawned, snake-like, until his whole head seemed to be made up of pink-ribbed flesh and white pointed teeth. Then he settled himself down on the warm brick like a hen upon her nest, folding his forepaws beneath his white, feathery bib. His great yellow eyes began to close as he let himself succumb once more to a blissful doze. Then all at once, his eyes were wide open again. His tail twitched away from his side and lashed the brick behind in slow motion. Something which only the cat could sense had stirred within the depths of one of the threatening caves, something which had metamorphosed from a glimmer among the shadows beneath the seventh arch into a white, rounded, shiny thing that was slowly emerging into the light of day. The Queen of the Termites? No, it was only the Velox being wheeled out into the yard by Spider Spinetti, in preparation for her annual overhaul. In three hours, her body would gleam like the baronial silver and her engine would purr as smoothly as the tom cat who, curiosity assuaged, was now settling down on the wall to watch Spider's efforts with the idle gaze of a baron observing his butler.

In less than a week Eddie and Maureen would be married, and Spider would be Eddie's best man. He would be chauffeuring the happy couple around Southend on their honeymoon. It had been the proudest moment of Spider's life when Eddie had asked him. But now there was a slight feeling of sadness when he thought forward to the day, especially after what Eddie had said to him only a few hours earlier, when Spider had dropped him off at the Mansions after his stag night at the Samson.

'Listen, Spider-of-mine,' drawled Eddie, leaning in through the window of the Velox, 'I don't know how to put this, but well… it's just that Reen and me really appreciate you driving us on our honeymoon.'

'Snuthin' Eddie,' snuffled Spider in reply, gripping the wheel with modest embarrassment.

'Oh yes, it is, mate,' blurted Eddie, bringing his fist down on the bonnet with such a boom that poor Spider almost hit the roof, 'I'll be honest son, I don't know what I'd 'ave done without you driving me an' all—and I haven't forgotten…'

Tears welled up in Eddie's eyes behind his shades, as his voice softened, and he warmed to his sentimental speech.

'…I haven't forgotten all that you've done for me in the past, so when we get back from Southend, the old girl's yours to keep,' said Eddie, affectionately patting the roof of the Velox. 'You've got a real touch with her, you have,' he croaked, starting to caress the Velox's bonnet with a sensuous touch, as if to soothe the throbbing caused by the thump, he had given it, a few moments before.

Spider had sat back with a stunned expression on his face.

'Eddie—you must be pissed mate!'

'Who you callin' pissed, sunshine?' bellowed Eddie, suddenly exploding into mock fury as he leaned in through the window and grabbed Spider by the lapels of his drape, 'I don't wanna hear any more about it, see?' said Eddie more gently now, letting Spider slump back into the leopard skin-lined interior. 'You've earned her mate, and if anybody can keep her on the road for the next twenty years, it's you. Now

I'm goin' to kip.'

At the bottom of the stairs, Eddie had turned and shouted, 'Oi Spider, get some fish hooks under them lapels.' Staggering up the first few steps, he began to sing: 'So, I climbed one, two flight, three flight, four...' but Spider didn't hear him – by the time Eddie reached the top, Spider was still staring at the dashboard of the Velox.

*

Spider hadn't guessed the real reason for Eddie's gift. His sadness was purely because he thought that his mentor had his eyes on a bigger motor – maybe a flash American job, Buick or Cadillac. And he was genuinely excited at the prospect of owning the Velox. It was just that he felt that a change in the status quo was about to take place: perhaps his intuition was signalling to him that it was going to be a bigger change than he currently expected. He also felt hurt deep down by the thought that Eddie might be pensioning him off—there had been no mention of him continuing as driver for Eddie's new car. Was it that in some way he hadn't measured up, not 'lived the life?'

Whatever it was, he definitely had a lump in his throat that Sunday afternoon as he stacked singles on the auto-drop spindle of his Dansette record player, and even the combined efforts of Gene Vincent, Eddie Cochran and Buddy Holly couldn't prevent the pride he took in his work from being tinged with melancholy. In fact, when 'Three Steps to Heaven' came on in the dusk, he could hardly prevent the tears from rolling as he drew the tarpaulin over the Velox for the last time before the wedding.

*

News of the Ted Wed of the decade travelled fast, first among the East End Teds, then spreading south of the river and west along the North Circular. In a couple of weeks, even the most far-flung corners of the country had got a whiff of what was going on, and preparations were being made. Drapes were pressed, chrome polished and quiffs sculpted anew. Young Teds practiced the double somersault and the cross-buttock jive roll with their bobby-socked partners. Old goats made sure they could still go down for a back-flip without coming up with a hernia. It was true that Eddie had his enemies, even among the Teds, and that in the past there had been no love lost between different Ted communities, but now almost every Ted wanted to be at the wedding to wish the couple well, and if not at the wedding itself, to be at the Samson afterwards, and if not at the Samson, then at Southend, for it was an open secret that Eddie and Maureen were honeymooning there. In short, there was to be a regular gathering of the clans, and a great excuse for the Teddy Boy Roar to be heard across the land.

*

Half a mile from Uncle Bruno's yard, where Spider was locking the gates behind him, a gathering of a different kind was taking place in the saloon bar of The Bloody Mary. Ranged rather uncomfortably around a table were the Turnbulls and the Caldecotts, with Doll hovering in the background like a maid at the Palace and little 'Enery smiling benignly into space, picturing in his mind's eye the humour of the situation.

'Cigar, Harry?' said Mr Turnbull, leaning across the table and offering a fat and prosperous looking Havana to old Mr Caldecott.

'No thank you, er... Charles. I don't smoke,' he replied with a disdainful twitch of his scrubby moustache. He had acquired an air of self-righteousness peculiar to those who, until very recently, have been on forty Player's Weights a day.

'Don't worry, Dad, I'll help you out,' said Eddie, plucking the Havana from under his father's nose. The smile on Mr Turnbull's face sagged as Ethel groped for her Silk Cut. Eddie leaned back, cigar in hand, looking rather revolutionary behind his shades.

'Allow me,' said Mr Turnbull, his unctuousness returning as he offered a light to Ethel who, fag in mouth, was now ferreting in her bag for her eternally elusive matches.

'Thanks, Chas,' said Eddie, accepting the light on his mother's behalf and leaving his father in a thick, pungent cloud of smoke as he returned to his seat. Once again Mr Turnbull's smile seemed on the point of disintegration.

'Ted, you make me ashamed sometimes,' said old Mr Caldecott picking up his empty glass, 'what sort of an example is that to Maureen and the twins?'

'Eh?' said Maureen, who hadn't been listening to the conversation. She was more concerned with the game of darts the twins were playing on the other side of the bar.

Eddie puffed unrepentantly on his cigar.

'Come on, Harry, 'ave another drink,' said Dawn,

pouring oil (or in this case, mild and bitter) on old Mr Caldecott's troubled waters.

'Maureen?' asked Dawn, picking up Maureen's empty glass, 'Him inside must have drunk that lager hours ago, if he's anything like his father!' She tittered self-consciously at her joke.

Maureen smiled and patted her swelling stomach. She had a soft spot for Dawn, who was Mr Turnbull's second wife: she was soft, blond and pneumatic— 'Wifey Mark II' Eddie called her. When he first met her, he'd said: 'She's got more of the Joan Sims about her than the Barbara Windsor.' As she looked at Dawn, Maureen remembered her own dead mother with respect, but not love. Small, fiery and ambitious, she had followed in the footsteps of the Windrush generation from Jamaica with her sights set on something more than the NHS or London Transport. She had split up with Maureen's father when their daughter was only two years old. She had then sought out and seduced Mr Turnbull, driving him rather unwillingly towards success in the surgical goods business, but the strain of whipping him on and keeping a household together for twenty years on a shoestring had helped to kill her. She hadn't had much time to spend with Maureen as she grew up, so she couldn't blame her stepfather for relaxing a little on Dawn's ample bosom now, and she didn't begrudge Dawn a slice of the cash which her own mother had, in large part, created.

'Another half won't do him any harm,' smiled Maureen, handing her glass to Dawn. Then she looked across at Eddie, who remained stolidly seated, puffing on his cigar and swilling beer, and she was glad he had gone his own way, even though he could be a pig at times.

'Nah, you sit down, Dawn—Ted'll get these, won't you son?' said old Mr Caldecott, phrasing the last three words as a command rather than a question.

'Oh,' said Dawn, hovering between sitting and standing for a few seconds until Maureen nudged Eddie into action and he began to get up.

'No, it's my shout,' said Mr Turnbull at the same moment, coming to the rescue of his wife. Eddie needed no persuading and sat down again, leaving Mr T. to hitch up his smile and make his way to the bar to buy his second round in succession.

'Gawd!' said old Mr Caldecott.

Two or three drinks passed. The Bloody Mary began to fill up with its Sunday night regulars. Smoke hung on the air like evening mist. The hubbub of voices swelled into a chorus as the stuffed birds looked out from their glass cases with permanent expressions of alarm. A piano began to jangle with a brassy sound which suggested the pianist wasn't so much 'tickling' its ivories as striking them with mailed fists. Brave voices rose in accompaniment and were carried along to the strains of 'Que Viva Espana' as Maureen took the twins back to the Mansions. The Turnbulls and the Caldecotts felt more relaxed around their table. Ethel fell asleep as old Mr Caldecott held forth on the cultivation of roses, while Dawn listened in rapt incomprehension. Charles Turnbull, seizing his moment, leaned towards Eddie and took hold of his arm with a chubby, confidential hand.

'The reception,' he said purposefully. 'Now I know you must be worried, but don't be—I've got everything under control. I've got you the very best, son.' Mr Turnbull leaned closer still and whispered, 'Maureen doesn't know anything about this yet, but I've hired the whole of the Oddfellows' Hall in Leytonstone...'

'Yes, I had heard,' said Eddie in a loud voice. Mr Turnbull looked crestfallen and rather taken aback.

'Does Maureen know then?' Eddie took pity on Mr Turnbull and shook his head. Mr T. looked relieved, and his face brightened. 'Because I've got Audrey's of Ongar to do the catering—you know, oat kwizeen and all that. You won't let on to her, will you son?'

'Cub's honour,' said Eddie, putting two fingers to the side of his head. Mr Turnbull looked relieved for a moment, but then he frowned and leaned forward again.

'Some very important people will be there, and...' Mr T. paused, casting around for words to express himself.

'Yeh?' replied Eddie, encouragingly.

'Well, you mustn't misunderstand me, but...' Charles Turnbull faltered again and began to work up a colour.

'Try me.'

'Well..., your... mates'

'Mates?' queried Eddie.

'I mean, they won't cause any trouble, will they?'

'Trouble?' replied Eddie ominously, though at the same time trying to suppress a broad grin. With marvellous control of his facial muscles, he managed to deepen his scowl.

'I don't know quite how to put this, but...'

'Don't worry, Mr T.' said Eddie with a confidential chuckle, 'I know exactly what you mean. You've laid out a lot of dough and you've got some big knobs coming you want to impress—am I right or am I right? But if by chance there's any aggravation,' he continued, aiming a playful punch at Mr Turnbull's chin, 'just have a word with my best man—he'll deal with it.'

Mr Turnbull looked a little (but not much) relieved and managed another smile.

'That's all I wanted to know, son. You're not offended, are you?' he said, taking Eddie's arm in a confidential grasp. Eddie shook his head and patted the hand on his arm.

'Who is your best man by the way? I'd like to meet him before the big day and discuss a few details.'

'Here's your chance, chief,' said Eddie, getting to his feet. 'Oi, Spider, over here mate.'

Not for the first time that evening the smile dropped from Charles Turnbull's face as he turned to see the diminutive figure of Spider Spinetti pushing his way towards him through the crowded bar.

'Gawd!' remarked old Mr Caldecott.

*

The last few days before the wedding disappeared in a welter of well-wishing drinks and last-minute arrangements, giving Eddie no time for sober reflection. But on the morning of the big day Maureen got up early, bathed, changed and left Eddie to sort himself out, knowing he would be an age.

After his bath, Eddie lay on his bed for a while with slices of cucumber on his eyes, his mind filled with small specks of light. At last, he got up, stretched, farted, approached the great hideous wardrobe and flung open the doors with his usual cavalier gesture. It was then that the first pangs hit him, sending him back a couple of steps and making him sit down heavily on the end of the bed. It was as if he had opened a fairy treasure chamber, crammed with enchanted jewels, their poignant splendour emphasized by the fact that they would soon vanish from his life like a mirage in the desert.

Drapes of every colour—sapphire, emerald and ruby— glowed in the shadows. Silver lamé sparkled here, gold there. Belt buckles and boot lace tie studs shone with the deep lustre of the finest pewter, and a carpet of crepe soles strewed the floor, with a few winklepickers gleaming among them like doubloons. A million memories fled through the open doors of the wardrobe, like spirits escaping from a spell, but a good few of them lodged in Eddie's mind. He stood up, reached out with a trembling hand, took the sleeve of a drape, and rubbed the material between his finger and thumb.

He took it out of the wardrobe and held it against himself in the mirror. It was made of bright yellow Harris Tweed, flecked with black and trimmed with a Prussian blue collar and cuffs. It had been given to him by a Hooray Henry as a token of his gratitude for Eddie's timely intervention in extracting him from a brawl at Pickett's Lock. The label on the inside pocket bore the name of Hooray's father and the address of his tailoring business on Savile Row.

Chuckling at the memory, Eddie slipped the jacket on over his bare shoulders and buttoned it in front to cover his wedding tackle, though he had to suck in his paunch to do so. He admired himself in the mirror, first from one side, then the other. He took out a matching ratter, crammed it on his head and pulled the peak well down over his eyes. He stuck his thumbs in his pockets, squared his shoulders and scowled at himself for a few moments.

'Nah.'

Now he stood naked before the drapes again, though this

time he reached much further into the past and pulled out a faded, threadbare memory. It was his very first drape jacket, the one he wore to see *Rock Around the Clock* at the Trocadero in the Elephant and Castle. Closing his eyes, he remembered that night. The delicious wait in the dark cinema, punctuated by the occasional shout, fart, curse or flare of a match. An ice cream falling out of the sky and landing on the bow wave sitting next to him. Tension mounting. The Teds were waiting, knowing that their time had come.

Then the drab flickering of film as a chubby, benign-looking man with a kiss curl smiled down from the screen—hardly a Che Guevara, but the thin clatter which flowed from his guitar and crackled out from the Troc's loudspeakers became the revolutionary anthem of its day. Within seconds, Teds were jiving in the aisles and showing their contempt for sitting down by symbolically slashing and ripping up seats.

It was no more than a sawn-off gabardine mac with velvet collars and cuffs sewn on, but Eddie could still picture the scene as his mother laboured long and painstakingly over that task, while his father huffed and puffed in the background, muttering about the war and a good spell in uniform. But this was Eddie's own uniform, being made right there on the kitchen table, and he was as proud to wear it as his father had been to wear his, a dozen years earlier—and as proud to return bruised and battered from the rumpus at the Trocadero as his father had been to return victorious from the war.

As the memories flowed, Eddie was seized with the wild notion that he might wear this ancient drape to the wedding and thus end his career as a Ted dressed as he had begun it, almost quarter of a century earlier. His hand shook as he extracted the drape from the wardrobe, sending a few moths fluttering towards the ceiling, but he could hardly squeeze his arms up the sleeves, and his dream was finally dispelled as he attempted to button it across his belly. The fragile stitches burst along almost every seam as the ancient drape burst open like a huge, over-ripe seed pod. Unimpeded by stitch or seam, the jacket now met across Eddie's paunch, and he began to button it mechanically, a horror-stricken look on his face.

Then he stopped, grinned and muttered 'Sorry Mum' under his breath before peeling off the shredded remains of the drape to stand naked yet again before the mirror. A moment later, Maureen stuck her head round the bedroom door to destroy Eddie's reverie once and for all.

'Come on, love, I'm not marrying you in your birthday suit—we're on in under an hour.'

In the end, Eddie chose a sober charcoal grey drape with maroon velvet collar and cuffs and matching maroon suede crepe-soled boppers. A frilly shirt and black bootlace tie completed the picture. Maureen had chosen a white jacket, pencil skirt, matching shoes and pillbox hat from which her jet black, straightened hair curved slightly forward into points beneath her chin. A few moments later, Spider was there on the doorstep, nervously resplendent in bottle green drape and an expertly sculpted bow wave which Eddie viewed with envious approval.

'We on then?' he asked, taking Maureen by the hand.

Spider nodded, tongue-tied and overawed by the momentous occasion.

'Twins ready, are they?'

'Ready, Eddie,' came the chorused reply from out on the balcony.

Eddie tossed the keys of the flat to Spider who twitched violently, but just managed to hold on to them.

'Right, that's it then,' said Eddie with an air of finality. Taking a deep breath, he strode out of the flat on the twentieth floor of the Mansions with Maureen on his arm.

Chapter 10

Summertime Blues

The three men playing cards in the yard should have finished their lunch break and gone back to work half an hour earlier—and it was Eddie's job to tell them so.

'Oi, Mikey—play time's over. Get your boys back to work pronto!'

Mikey, a seasoned expert at trying it on, looked up at Eddie's open office window and grinned defiantly, displaying his lack of front teeth. The two young men, Mikey's apprentices, smirked at one another. But Eddie, like a fat trout on a hot afternoon, didn't rise to the bait. He hadn't even come to the window to shout his instructions. Now he put his feet up on his desk, clasped his hands behind his head and gazed up at the ceiling.

Mikey felt cheated. To show his contempt he rolled his tongue, stuck it out through the gap in his teeth and, with the precision of an archerfish, squirted brown saliva at a target in the dust known only to himself. The two young ones sniggered briefly until they realised that Mikey wasn't amused.

The heat sat on Turnbull's of Bow like a fat, hairy backside, weighing down the workforce. The weak breeze that was wafting up from the canal was as warm and smelly as fart gas and provided no respite. Eddie wiped the sweat from his forehead and shiny crown, but almost at once tiny pinpricks of moisture reappeared, swelling into droplets which fused with their neighbours before rolling away down the greasy slopes of his head. One droplet found the gap between Eddie's eyebrows where it ran under the bridge created by a pair of aviator spectacles before glissading down the side of his nose and coming to rest in the thick underbrush of a Zapata moustache. Another found easier passage past Eddie's right eyebrow, pausing only briefly on his cheekbone before rolling unimpeded over smooth flesh where a prodigious mutton chop sideburn had once sprouted.

A third meandered across Eddie's crown, which was now almost completely bald, and trickled down the back of his neck, a route that was no longer being barred by the massive duck's arse which had once protruded there. The remaining hair had been cropped into a neat Boston just above the collar of his white nylon shirt.

It had been over a year since the wedding, a bad year in which all of Eddie's carefully laid plans had come to fruition, but the fruit itself had turned to ashes in his mouth. Nowadays, he survived solely on the thin gruel of memory, a meal which he had ample time to consume in his capacity as chief under-manager at Turnbull's of Bow.

Every day the ceiling of his office became a screen onto which his mind projected his thoughts through the unseeing lenses of his eyes. These daily home movies invariably included shots of the wedding and honeymoon, as often as not beginning with the moment when Eddie stepped out of the flat in the Mansions for the last time with Maureen on his arm. That day and the precious few which had followed had been among the happiest of Eddie's life, so it wasn't surprising that memories of this period tended to take precedence over all the others in Eddie's private picture show, though one incident which took place when the new football season started was still so raw in Eddie's memory, and it filled him with such shame and guilt that he forced himself to look at it again and again,

Maureen could no longer go with the twins to watch the Hammers at Upton Park unless she could find someone reliable to look after baby John when she was away. Her definition of 'reliable person' didn't include Eddie who was drunk or asleep for most of the time at weekends. She had persuaded Dawn to babysit on occasion, but one afternoon the twins were desperate to go to an important cup game, and she had to take baby John to Whipps Cross hospital because he was suffering from an infection.

'Come on, Eddie, please. The twins are still too young to go on their own, especially with all the skins in the ground,' pleaded Maureen, trying to keep her anger under control.

'I don't like football,' grunted Eddie sullenly.

'Eddie—please,' said Maureen, 'I know it was tough for you when you were a Ted, but now that you look like... THAT... you'll be able to keep them out of a fight.'

Eddie didn't reply, instead pouring himself another whisky and opening the paper to cover his face.

Maureen finally lost it: 'You lazy fat fuck,' she screamed, 'you fucking apology for a man.' Baby John began to bawl as Maureen wrestled the pram out into the hallway and through the front door.

The twins glowered at Eddie and made their own attempt at persuading him until he fell asleep. Then they slipped out of the house.

When Maureen returned from a long and draining trip to the hospital, she found the twins sitting on the doorstep, with their heads bowed.

'What are you two doing down there?' she shouted, waking baby John who began to bawl again. When the twins looked up, Maureen saw that their faces were bruised and cut. They hadn't even managed to get into the ground. They had been beaten up and robbed by a gang of young skins in a side street.

'Sorry, Mum,' they muttered.

'Don't you two idiots be sorry,' said Maureen through clenched teeth, 'It's him who will be sorry.'

Eddie lay slumped on the living room sofa, with the newspaper over his face. Maureen whisked it off and slapped him hard, sending his aviators flying across the room.

'You whaaat!' he grunted, staggering to his feet and pushing Maureen who replied with two more slaps to his face. As Eddie raised his fist, the twins, brave as lions, leaped between them, their bruised bodies crying out in pain as they did so. At the sight of their young, battered faces, Maureen felt her rage at Eddie begin to ebb away to be replaced by love and sympathy for her sons, while Eddie began to feel the deep sense of shame that he was still feeling months later as he projected the memories onto the office ceiling.

When he remembered upsetting episodes like this, Eddie usually soothed himself by returning to fonder memories from happier days. But that afternoon Eddie passed his hand over the stubble on the back of his neck, and at once a horrifying image appeared on the ceiling, one that, try as he might, he felt compelled to watch.

It was a man in white who was grinning fiendishly as he bent over Eddie with a whirring electric clipper in his hand. For a moment, Eddie gazed at his own image in the mirror opposite, the last image of his former life before the shades were plucked unceremoniously from his nose, plunging him into a blur of bright lights and dim shapes as if his head had been thrust underwater.

'Can't give you a proper haircut in these, can we, my son?' enthused the barber.

When the shades were reinstated, they sat upon an object which closely resembled a huge, putty-coloured, shiny egg. The barber was standing behind the egg, comb and clippers in hand, beaming down upon his creation.

'Now ain't that a sight for sore eyes?' he gloated.

Eddie stared dully at his new self with nothing more than casual interest. Only when two kids, walking behind him with their mother, sniggered and whispered, 'Humpty Dumpty sat on a wall,' did he realise for the first time what he had done. Then he blinked and the apparitions fled, leaving him standing on the balcony outside his old flat in the Mansions with Maureen beside him. Although he had conjured it up in his mind's eye many times before, the vision once more brought tears to his eyes, just as it had for the first time on the morning of his wedding.

*

The balcony had been transformed from a dingy catwalk into an aisle of vibrant colour. The rusty balustrade and stained concrete were draped with a mass of old Silver Jubilee bunting, fluttering gaily in the bright April breeze. Queenie smiled her royal blessing on the happy couple from scores of plastic Union Jacks as Eddie and Maureen took their first steps along the roll of remaindered red carpet from Allied of Romford. The next moment the skies opened and unleashed a deluge of paper rain as the children, who had been waiting and whispering on the balcony above for the past hour, hurled down handfuls of homemade confetti amid wild hoots and howls of pent-up excitement. The coloured paper settled on what remained of Eddie's oily hair, so that by the time he reached the lift at the end of the balcony he looked as if he was wearing an exotic, flowery bathing hat. The twins held open the lift gates as Eddie and Maureen dashed inside, hotly pursued by Spider and the honeymoon baggage.

The lift had also been transformed, this time by the Mansions' graffiti artists, turning the drab aluminium box into an enormous greetings telegram. The walls, ceiling and even the floor were adorned with black cats, four leafed clovers and horseshoes, together with some more X-rated images and symbols.

For a few silent moments, the five of them looked at each other in the battered old mirror that made up one wall of the lift. Then, somewhere around the fifteenth floor, Maureen and the twins burst into uncontrollable fits of laughter. Eddie, rightly suspecting that his flowery bathing hat was partly responsible for the merriment, coloured up and scowled at Spider, daring him to so much as raise a smile, but by the tenth floor, he too was laughing 'til the tears ran and even Spider was grinning sheepishly as the lift touched bottom with a bump.

*

At this point, the phone on Eddie's desk rang, making him shoot upright in his chair and extinguishing the images on the ceiling as if someone had pulled the plug on the projector. Eddie lifted the receiver mechanically and registered the first few words of the message which then turned into a kind of drone, as of a chain saw deep in the woods.

'Yeah, yeah—keep your hair on.'

When the droning stopped, he replaced the receiver and looked up at the ceiling again.

Time passed but at first no pictures appeared.

The heat pressed in on Eddie's head, squeezing juice from every pore as if from a lemon held in a slowly closing vice. Then, in a slow, subtle transformation, the dirty cream of the office ceiling began to change into a pale, shiny lime green, and the cold sweat on Eddie's face became hot tears running down his cheeks. His gaze wandered slowly down the wall of the hospital ward, every crack and indentation of which was now familiar to him through long hours of minute examination, coming to rest at last on the tiny shrunken head stuck like a button in the middle of an enormous white pillow.

The doctors had said that Ethel Caldecott's cancer was inoperable, but they had pumped her full of blood and given her a colostomy to prolong her life. When Eddie had seen her for the first time after the operation, he had wished that she could have been allowed to pass away peacefully in the little back room in Paragon Road. He was all too aware of her lifelong horror of hospitals and surgery, and her obstinate refusal to see a doctor, even when it became obvious that she was very ill.

But Ethel was a fighter. When she did wake up in that alien environment which she had feared for so long, she found to her surprise and joy that it was populated by warm and caring people just like herself. With their help, she adapted herself to the pain and difficulties of her situation with courage and determination.

'It's only a matter of time, I'm afraid,' the specialist had said, but as soon as Eddie had witnessed his mother begin her struggle to hang on to life, he hoped and prayed—but dared not think—that this 'matter of time' might be weeks rather than days, maybe even months. And so it turned out, for it was now almost a year since the operation and Ethel had been well enough to return to Paragon Road. But in the last few days her condition had suddenly deteriorated, and she had been rushed into hospital again. Eddie had visited her the night before, and it was the memory of that visit that he was now revisiting on the office ceiling that hot August afternoon.

A long, sighing exhalation ending in a brief, staccato rattle warned Eddie that his mother was surfacing from one of her deep, drugged sleeps.

'Mum, Mum, it's Ted here.'

There was no response. He leaned closer to the tiny head.

'How're you doing today, Mum?'

Still nothing. Then very slowly the face inclined towards him.

'You're looking better today,' he continued in a whisper, because his voice had begun to quaver and crack with emotion. The suggestion of a smile appeared at the corners of Ethel's mouth and flickered across her eyelids. Though her eyes remained closed, her lips parted very slightly.

'Ted? Ooo, an' I was havin' such a nice dream too,' she sighed. 'Is Harry up yet? 'Has he fed Tina?'

'No, well maybe—he'll be along any moment, Mum.'

'I was dreamin' of Tina—she's not still there, is she?'

'Er—sorry. Where?'

'On the bed of course. She jumped up and started makin' dough—you know how she does—but she was all plump and fluffy like she was ten years younger and…and her eyes were shining…and her fur was sort of glowing…and it was…blue!'

'Blue?'

'Yes Ted—a wonderful kind of blue, like… like… well, it was like… like…'

Ethel's voice trailed away so that Eddie thought she was returning to sleep. Then her eyes flicked open, and she suddenly sat upright. Her skull was almost bald from the radiation treatment, and her staring eyes, toothless gums and the white sheet pulled up to her neck made her look like something that might rear up at you from the shadows of the Ghost Train or the Haunted House at the Kursaal. If Eddie hadn't witnessed this before, he would have winced at Ethel's shriek, which silenced the subdued murmurings around the rest of the ward.

'Ted! You're not my Ted. Go away whoever you are…Harry, Harry, tell him to go away!' screeched Ethel, staring wildly around her. 'I'll, I'll…' the words died away in her throat as she got her bearings and remembered what had happened to her—and to her son. With a sigh, she sank back onto the pillow. 'Sorry, Ted, but I just can't get used to the way you look nowadays. I wish you'd wear your old clothes and grow your hair a bit. Sometimes I think you're a burglar with a stocking mask on—honest I do! Anyway, you should be with Maureen, not with me. She needs you more than I do, with the baby an' all.'

'Reen can look after 'erself, Mum,' answered Eddie rather bitterly.

Ethel began to knead the sheets with worry after her outburst. 'God knows what Mrs Barnaby's going to say now.'

But Mrs Barnaby wasn't going to say anything. Her bed was empty. She had been tidied away along with her bits and pieces into one of the cubicles in the corridor immediately outside the ward where very sick patients were taken. Eddie had seen her on his way in and had said 'Hello,' but the big, strong, blustering woman had been withering more swiftly than the flowers Eddie had brought her a few days before – her eyes had been open when he arrived with them, but she had given him no reply or sign of recognition.

'Harry! Well, I never!'

Eddie looked up and saw his father—or rather he saw his father's hands because the rest of him was obscured by an enormous, dripping bunch of blood red roses.

'How's my gel tonight, then?' came old Mr Caldecott's muffled voice.

'Hang about, Dad, and I'll get you some'ing to put them in,' said Eddie, taking the flowers from his father and setting off in search of a vase, glad to have an excuse to leave his parents together. When he returned, he found that Harry had taken Ethel in his arms. Eyes closed, Ethel's face shone above old Mr Caldecott's shoulder like a full moon on a warm summer's night. Eddie had never seen such an expression of serene contentment. He stopped, not daring to come any closer in case he disturbed the tableau. Then, to his profound horror and disbelief, a bell rang loud in his ear to signal the end of visiting time.

'Oh, come on—he's only just arrived, for God's sake,' Eddie protested, turning to look for the ward sister. But although the bell rang again, the ward itself had disappeared. 'Sod it,' he whispered, rubbing his eyes and reaching for the phone on his desk.

'That you, Eddie? Look, we've got about 'alf a ton of trusses down here at the gate. If you blokes can't shift 'em by the time the guv'nor gets back, there's going to be some aggravation, son-in-law or no son-in-law, know what I mean?'

'All right, all right, Stanley—keep your 'air on mate. The cavalry's on the way,' said Eddie, hanging up the phone. He stretched, swung his feet off the desk and crossed the office to the open window. Mikey and his sidekicks were playing cards in the yard below.

'Oi, Mikey! Get your lads down to the gate and do some shiftin', pronto!' shouted Eddie. Mikey didn't move. His apprentices smirked at one another. 'Oi, Mikey—I mean right now!'

This time Mikey drew back his sleeve and tapped his watch to indicate the time, then looked up with a toothless, triumphant grin and shook his head.

'All right, as soon as tea break's over, get me?' grunted Eddie and slammed the window shut, immediately regretting doing so because he had shut the oven door on himself and wouldn't now be able to open it again without losing face. Once more his only escape lay in the office ceiling, and like a man dying of thirst in the desert who conjures mirages of tinkling fountains from the burning sands, he looked up and within a few moments he was filling his lungs with fresh spring air.

*

Eddie and Maureen dashed from the lift hand in hand, still laughing until what they saw across the estate made them stop and draw breath with amazement. The Velox stood proudly at the head of a column of vintage cars which seemed to stretch the length of Paragon Road. In among the Zodiacs, Crestas and Consuls stood their flashy American cousins—Buicks, Plymouths and Oldsmobiles—like Texas oilmen in Stetsons standing in a queue of flat caps and ratters.

'Come on,' said Spider, taking the best manly initiative for the first time that day. Maureen and Eddie needed no further prompting, for at the same moment the kids from the Mansions, who had pursued the lift down twenty flights, burst through the doors at the bottom of the staircase. A cacophony of car horns urged the happy couple on in their race to the Velox. A cheer and a flurry of ratters hurled high into the air indicated that they had beaten the kids by a short head. However, a moment later the cheers turned into shouts of alarm as the pursuers changed tack and aimed their supply of rice and confetti at the large number of very satisfactory secondary targets in the shape of Teds lounging against their cars. In the ensuing minutes, a good deal of cool was lost in diving for cover or running in pursuit of snatched ratters, but at last all the Teds regained their machines and the column moved slowly off, led proudly by Spider at the wheel of the Velox.

'Oh blimey, where'd you dig that 'orrible lot up?' chuckled Eddie, secretly pleased and touched at the turnout, 'and who told the Old Bill to stay at 'ome then?'

'Li'l birdie,' said Spider cockily.

'I thought they'd have this lot wrapped up in a big brown paper parcel by now,' Eddie went on, jerking his thumb over his shoulder to indicate the cavalcade behind.

'Dad'll throw a fit for sure,' said Maureen, unable to suppress a smile at the prospect. The twins drummed on their knees with glee.

'Don't worry, darlin',' said Eddie, throwing one comforting paw round Maureen while picking some blossom out of his hair with the other, 'they're nice lads really.'

But even as Eddie spoke, Spider saw in the rear-view mirror that, according to plan, the first cars had begun to peel off the column and disappear into side streets, so that by the time they got to Beckford Registry Office, they were alone. Eddie stepped out of the Velox, ready to regale his guests with a few well-chosen lines, but then turned to Spider for an explanation when he saw the empty street behind them. His best man replied with a theatrical wink while Maureen looked surprised but rather relieved. As for the twins, they looked downright fed up. Mr Turnbull, beaming on the steps of the Registry Office, was none the wiser.

'Ah, good morning, Mr Turnbull, lovely day for it, what?' said Spider, grasping Mr T. by the hand. 'You're looking very dapper, sir, if you don't mind me saying so—and I think Mrs Turnbull looks a picture.' He stooped to kiss the back of Dawn's gloved hand.

'Well, I never,' said Dawn, giggling with delight.

'Oily sod. I'll 'ave 'im later,' whispered Eddie as he too

had to kiss the proffered hand of Dawn Turnbull, whose taste for this form of greeting had been whetted now. 'Here,' he whispered, raising his lips from the white glove, 'where's all the relatives, then?'

'Oh, it was Charlie's idea. He wanted this to be your moment—yours and Reen's that is—don't worry, you'll 'ave a belly full of them later,' said Dawn, rolling her eyes.

At that moment, Eddie felt deeply touched and at the same time grateful that the Teds had disappeared. Until then, he hadn't begun to think about how much difference a few words in a registry office might make to the commitment he had felt towards Maureen for the past ten years or so. After the short service, he knew he had been wrong as he sat with Maureen in the back seat of the Velox on the way to the Oddfellows Hall. He felt happy, but also rather ashamed deep down, not at the tears which once again welled up beneath his shades as Spider passed him the ring, but that he had kept Maureen waiting so long before taking the vows. Nobody spoke very much. Even the twins were quite subdued, though not in a sad or gloomy way. They had all been moved by what had just been said and witnessed.

'You'd better stick that on before you go into the reception,' said Spider, tossing a brand-new ratter into Eddie's lap, 'we don't want you wearing flowers in your hair again, do we? People might think you're a blooming hippie or some'ing.'

'Thinks of everything, don't he,' said Eddie, reaching forward and patting Spider on the shoulder, 'quite the best little best man. Cheeky sod!' Everybody laughed, including Eddie, though he couldn't help but be impressed by Spider's coming-of-age.

*

Eddie leaned against a wall in the far corner of the Oddfellows Hall, loosened his tie and tried to look inconspicuous. This was, of course, quite impossible, but luckily most of the guests weren't overly anxious to make his acquaintance, except when Mr Turnbull decided that an introduction was essential. Swiftly and furtively, Eddie transferred three tiny vol-au-vents from the plate in his left hand to his mouth, scarcely pausing to chew the morsels before washing them down with champagne. Already he felt acid bile rising in his throat as the brew in his stomach began to bubble and ferment.

'Oi, Spider,' hissed Eddie, waylaying his best man as he hurried by on some solicitous errand, 'ain't there any other booze or nosh? I've been eating for half an hour and I'm still ravenous. I must have had about sixteen of these things, but the fizzy stuff keeps making them repeat—I can feel them all bouncing about at the back of me throat, like ping pong balls at a Bingo session.'

'Oh dear,' said Spider, 'Audrey WOULD be miffed to hear you say that Eddie.'

'Audrey? Who's she when she's at home cookin' chips?'

'HE is the bloke who created all these "ping pong balls" and the rest. This is Oat Kwizeen, boss,' said Spider jauntily.

'Yeah? Well, I could do with a proper pint. What happened to the lads anyway? They'd have a few cans with 'em.'

Not for the first time that day Spider gave Eddie one of his infuriating theatrical winks, then disappeared into the crowd. Eddie was about to follow, but the deep-seated horror of being introduced to people restrained him. He felt safer with his back to the wall. 'Bloated budgerigars,' he muttered, then bit ferociously into a roll of ham in which Audrey had cunningly concealed a gout of mayonnaise, half of which hit the back of his throat, while the other half spattered the lapel of his drape. He looked up quickly to see the faces of guests who had been watching his antics with horrified fascination turning hastily away. Nibbling was definitely not Eddie's forte.

'Try one of these, love—for special guests.'

It was Maureen who had magically appeared from the melee with Gladstone Morgan on one arm and Gladstone's wife Vanetta on the other. She was carrying a tray covered with a white cloth, one corner of which she lifted to reveal a cache of beef patties still hot from the oven.

'You're an angel,' said Eddie, who paused just long enough to give Gladstone a big hug and to kiss Vanetta's hand before stuffing the first pattie into his mouth.

'I'm made up to see you, Graves—and you Vanetta,' said Eddie through the mouthful, 'sorry about this 'orrible lot and the 'music,' if you can call it that—hope Percy Dalton is treating you well, Graves? Let's have a beer sometime soon, mate.'

Eddie just had time to push another pattie into his pocket before Maureen and her two special guests disappeared into the crowd.

A ripple of applause from the other end of the hall signalled that the jazz band had come to the end of its rather tired set of renditions of old Acker Bilk and Kenny Ball numbers. Dressed in ludicrous pink tuxedos, the five portly and aging members of the group trudged off and disappeared through a gap in the gold satin curtains at the back of the stage.

Guests nibbled, sipped and mingled. Mr Turnbull, who had been steering the mayor's wife around the dance floor, spotted Eddie through a gap in the crowd, and before his partner could escape, he suggested she should come and meet his new son-in-law. Eddie saw the move and took evasive action by diving into the thickest part of the crowd. 'Where the bleeding hell does he find them all,' he muttered, pushing and 'scuse me-ing' his way through the press of people until at last he came across two familiar faces.

'Doll—you've got to hide me. I'm being chased by me new father-in-law and the mayor's old woman. ''Allo 'Enery.'

'Hello, Eddie—and congratulations son,' said the little blind man, immaculate as ever in a grey morning suit, a pink carnation in his lapel, 'enjoying yourself, then?'

'I tell you what Henry—I'd rather be in the Mary suppin' a pint.'

'Eddie—what a thing to say,' tutted Doll, but she was clearly secretly pleased. 'Do I get to kiss the bridegroom, then?'

'Nah—it's not that bad really, 'specially now I've met you two,' said Eddie, throwing a big paw round Doll, closing his eyes and offering her his pouted lips: 'It could just do without the fish food and the Strangers on the Shore,' he chuckled, indicating the jazz band in their pink tuxedos who were filing zombie-like back onto the stage. A puzzled expression began to spread across Eddie's face as he took a closer look at the band. Even from halfway back in the hall,

140

they looked different somehow. There was something weirdly familiar about them now.

'When did you say the little one is due, Eddie?' asked Doll.

'It can't be,' answered Eddie in a faraway voice, shading his eyes.

'Eddie?'

'Eh, what... Sorry Doll, miles away. September, I think—yeah, the end of September. Look, will you both excuse me a mo'—I've just got to check up on some'ing.'

'Doesn't change,' said Doll, shaking her head as she watched Eddie pushing his way through the crowd to the front of the stage.

'It bleedin' well is!' croaked Eddie as the band leader approached the microphone.

'Afternoon ladies and gents,' boomed an echoing and highly amplified voice. 'We're the Flyin' Saucers and we bring congratulations from Mars, Uranus and everyone at the Samson to Eddie and Maureen on their wedding day. We'd like to thank our support band, the Lounge Lizards, for getting' you in the mood—and we'll try to get you out of that particular mood as quickly as we can, startin' with our very own signature tune. A-one, a-two, a one, two, three, four...'

'Oh Gawd.' Somewhere in the Oddfellows Hall, Mr Caldecott's voice was drowned out by the thunderous opening bars of Billy Lee Riley's "Flying Saucers Rock and Roll" as a score of Teds and their girls emerged from behind the gold satin curtains and started bopping furiously. Eddie looked round to find Spider standing beside him. The best man produced his biggest wink of the day and handed Eddie a can of beer.

'You little darlin',' laughed Eddie, scooping Spider up and carrying him through the pandemonium to the front of the stage where Dotun and Delroy, resplendent in African wax print drapes, were twirling and lifting their girlfriends with nonchalant ease.

*

The pictures on the office ceiling became blurred, just as they had in Eddie's memory. Familiar faces chased one another across the paintwork, looming up and rushing away like images on a gigantic fruit machine. Mr Turnbull about to erupt. Willie without his Wig. Spider without his drainpipes. Then Charles Turnbull again, this time looking like a bright sunny day with his tie loosened and a great deal of liquor under his belt.

Eddie tried to focus his eyes on one particular scene, but the pictures began to speed up and merge with one another. Little 'Enery's enigmatic smile as he guided Doll across the dance floor with effortless ease. Dotun's face, upside down, as he played the piano at the Samson standing on his head. The twins hooting and waving as they flashed by on the rollercoaster at the Kursaal in Southend. People running past them on the pier seeking shelter from an approaching storm. The pictures ran faster and faster until their colours blurred into a greyish white, like the miraculous flakes of snow which blew into their faces as they walked along the beach on the last day of their honeymoon.

'You wouldn't believe we were sunbathin' yesterday would you Reen?' laughed Eddie, turning to kiss his wife. But the snow had drawn a discreet bridal veil across

Maureen's face, and soon the pale shadow that was the rest of her also vanished, leaving Eddie alone in the blizzard.

'Reen?' he shouted, but his voice was reduced to a whisper by the furious wind. Despite the cold, he felt sweat forming between his shoulder blades and trickling down his spine.

'R-e-e-e-en?' he wailed, wiping the mixture of snow and sweat from his face and straining his eyes into the storm. 'For Christ's sake Reen, where are you?'

Then, as if the whirling drum of the fruit machine of memories had come to an abrupt stop, there was Maureen's face staring up at him. It was grey and shaking slightly in its frame of black hair.

'I—I don't understand Eddie, why are we here? You haven't...'

'Yes darling, it's a wedding present,' said Eddie, bestowing a kiss to which Maureen did not respond. 'It's our new home.'

They were standing outside the porch of No. 16 in a genteel cul-de-sac of 1930s semis in Willow Close, a quiet, residential area of Theydon Bois, where cherry trees grew out of the pavement at regular intervals.

'Let's go in and look around,' said Eddie, producing a key, but before he could put it in the lock the front door opened and out stepped Mr Turnbull, beaming beneficently. Dawn was just behind him.

'Well, if it isn't our two lovebirds returned to the nest,' he said, holding out his arms in greeting. There was a loud groan from the twins.

'Dad?' gasped Maureen, amazed for a moment only. Then her jaw began to clench as a frown of comprehension

143

cast its shadow over her face. 'Dad... what are you doin'
'ere?'

'Welcoming you to your new home of course, love,' said
Charles Turnbull, moving as if to embrace his stepdaughter.
Maureen retreated.

'Yeah, but what are you doin' in our new 'ome if that's
what it is?'

'Well... just tidying up a bit, you know, getting things
straight. Anyway, let's not hang around out here. Come in
and have a cup of tea.'

Maureen didn't move.

'Dad, did you buy this place for us?'

'Oh! come on now love, what sort of way is that to thank
Eddie. Come and have a cup of tea.'

'Dad! This is important. I'm not having any bleedin'
cups of tea until I've got a straight answer. Did you...?'

'All right, no I didn't. Now let's stop all this can we
please?'

'Well, if you didn't buy the place you must've put up a
bleedin' big pile of cash, otherwise we wouldn't have a hope
of paying the mortgage,' shouted Maureen as net curtains
began to twitch in Willow Close and alarmed white faces
peeped out—this was a 'nice' neighbourhood.

'Ah, that's where you're wrong my girl. Now, I expect
Eddie was keeping this as a surprise for you—like this lovely
home—but I'm sure he won't mind me telling you now.
Eddie's got a new job.'

'New job?'

'Yes,' said Mr Turnbull, beaming again and sticking his
thumbs in his waistcoat pockets. 'No more gravedigging for
him. Your Eddie's working for me now.'

Maureen turned slowly to face Eddie who was shifting guiltily from one foot to the other—this wasn't the way he had planned things at all. He shrugged.

'It's a good job, Reen,' he mumbled, in answer to Maureen's astonished, quizzical stare.

'Now I've heard it all!' she bellowed at last, then pushed past Eddie and waved the twins before her back up the path. 'Come on you lot—and you Eddie—we're going home to the Mansions to talk this over before we do anything else. How do you think me and the twins—or any black people, never mind our baby – are goin' to feel in a neighbourhood like this, eh?' she said, calmly now and looking around her in Willow Close. Several elderly white women, together with two or three builders who had been fixing the roof of a house further down the Close, had begun to gather on the other side of the road. Net curtains were no longer twitching instead, they had been drawn aside to allow an unimpeded view of the argument developing outside No.16.

'How do you think I'm going to feel coming out of me front door every morning with this lot checkin' me over,' she said, her voice rising and jerking her thumb over her shoulder to indicate the little crowd, 'never mind coming back on me own, or with the twins—or with a pram?'

She marched up the path to where the Velox was parked and where the twins were standing, hands on hips. They had already made their minds up. 'Eddie,' commanded Maureen.

'Daaad,' insisted the twins.

Eddie opened his mouth to speak, then paused in the hope that his father-in-law might somehow ventriloquize for him. But when no words came, he looked round for guidance. Mr Turnbull's face had gone a mushroom colour—this wasn't the way he had planned things either.

'Go on son, you'd better tell her,' he said in a husky voice, turning away and rubbing the back of his neck. Eddie faced Maureen again.

'There ain't no Mansions any more, Reen.' The words came tumbling out like constipation suddenly relieved.

'What you talking about "there ain't no Mansions?" Don't tell me they've fallen down or burned to the ground while we've been away?'

'No, nothing like that, love—it's just that we're here now, not there. I… I thought you'd be pleased.'

'All your stuff's here now, love,' Charles Turnbull whispered, 'we moved it while you were in Southend.'

'Don't worry, Reen,' Dawn chimed in, trying to sound cheerful, 'I packed up all your things meself.'

Maureen raised her fists as if she was about to box the three people before her, then let them drop to her sides as if to say, 'All right, you win.' Head bowed, she began to walk slowly down the path towards No.16.

'We did it for you, Reen,' implored Eddie as Maureen brushed past him. She turned, looked up at him, and answered in a quiet measured voice.

'How can you be so sure of that when you didn't ask me what I wanted in the first place?' She didn't pause for a reply but continued down the path.

'Reen?' said Eddie in a dazed voice, 'Look Reen, I… I've gotta pop out for an hour or so, tidy things up, you know. I'll see you later, all right?'

In reply, Maureen hunted in her bag, then ran back up the path towards Eddie, holding out a £5 note.

"Ere, you can get me some fags while you're out—

sixty'll do to start with.'

'Fags?'

'Yes, fuckin' FAGS,' shouted Maureen, stuffing the £5 note into the breast pocket of Eddie's jacket.

'But...' Eddie wanted to say something else—anything else—but all that came out was 'What about the baby?'

'To hell with the bloody baby,' screamed Maureen and ran into the house to hide her tears, pushing aside the feeble, imploring hands held out to her.

She hadn't smoked for ten years.

*

Eddie remembered the events of the next few hours with extreme clarity. He felt as if he had stepped outside himself and was watching from a distance like an impartial observer as he drove mechanically to the street in Beckford where he had parked and locked the Velox, then posted the keys to Spider. He took out the keys to a second-hand Granada which was parked behind the Velox, unlocked the boot and removed a suitcase which he carried into the nearby Gents. There he changed into a fitted shirt, flared jeans, white trainers and a bomber jacket. He packed his drape, drains and crepes in the suitcase which he threw into a skip behind the Gents. He drove to the barber's, sat like a zombie through the shearing, then walked round the corner to the optician where he exchanged the shades for tinted aviator glasses.

When the new Eddie emerged and began to climb into the Granada, his crepe-soled alter ego, which had been standing outside the shop with its nose pressed against the plate glass, leapt in beside him before he could slam the door and, in a few minutes, had re-entered the body which was its old and only home. Immediately Eddie was seized with a burning desire to see Maureen again, to show her what he had done, like a sinner yearning for the confessional.

At that point, the reality of Eddie's surroundings started to intrude into the projection, so that he perceived the past events as though they had happened on a much hotter day. For instance, he began to sweat heavily as he drove back towards Theydon Bois. He rolled the Granada's window down, but not so much as a breath of air crept inside. Then he grappled with the unfamiliar fan control on the dash board, but only succeeded in increasing the heat. The back of his neck stung furiously where the barber's cruel shears had laid the flesh bare. His eyes smarted from the salty sweat and mixed with the rivulets of tears that were already flowing down his cheeks. The hair clippings which had dropped down his collar made his neck and shoulders feel as if they were being brushed lightly with stinging nettles, and to complete his discomfort, the aviator specs began to steam up and slip down his nose.

When he finally did arrive at Willow Close, he found to his horror that the act of getting out of the Granada did not bring any relief from the heat. He staggered down the garden path like the soldier drowning in a sea of green gas he had once read about in a poem at school,

He stood for a moment in the porch, gasping for air, while he weighed up his chances of pressing the bell push, which somehow seemed very far away. He only succeeded with a supreme effort. The bell rang, two short bursts, though he only pressed it once, then again—and again. Eddie swayed gently while the bell continued to ring unaided. At last, the door opened, and Maureen popped out like a cuckoo from a clock and screamed at the sight of her transformed new husband, before popping back inside again, slamming the door in Eddie's face. But the bell kept ringing in two short bursts, and Maureen kept popping in and out until Eddie sat upright in his office chair, and the vision promptly disappeared.

*

The phone on Eddie's desk was ringing again. The office was stiflingly hot. He shook his head to dislodge the last elements of his waking nightmare and the puddles of sweat which had formed on his upturned face. He lifted the receiver.

'Caldecott?'

It was Charles Turnbull in a state of extreme agitation. He had taken to calling his son-in-law by his surname when his performance didn't meet with his approval. The habit made Eddie prickle with rage.

'What the bloody hell do you think you're playing at Caldecott? Stanley here says he rang you three hours ago to shift...'

Eddie put the receiver gently back on the hook. Something had begun to boil up inside him, making his windpipe contract to stop his heart from fluttering out of his mouth. He stood up, fastened the middle button of his jacket, then walked slowly downstairs and out into the yard where Mikey's two sidekicks were still bent over the orange box, intent on their game of cards. When Eddie approached, they bent lower still, and although he couldn't see their faces, he knew they were smirking.

The dull sound of skulls contacting each other at speed briefly disturbed the oppressive stillness of the afternoon. Eddie's windpipe relaxed a little as he turned away from the two unconscious bodies at his feet and strode towards the Gents.

'Mikey?' thundered Eddie from the doorway.

Mikey was standing at the urinal as he often did when he wasn't playing cards or drinking tea. He had been in the process of doing up his flies, but the sound of Eddie's furious voice struck such terror into him that his hand twitched involuntarily, and the steel teeth of his zip sank themselves agonisingly into his member before he had withdrawn it to safety.

Observing the resulting contortions, Eddie abandoned his original plan, deciding that Mikey's discomfort would be greater if he remained conscious. Instead, he turned on his heel and headed towards the main gate, leaving the Gents echoing with Mikey's piteous screams of pain. Seeing Eddie coming, Mr Turnbull emerged from his office, ready to do battle.

'Now look, Caldecott, I've got a bloody business to run here, you know. I…'

His sentence was left hanging in the air as Eddie walked straight past his father-in-law as if he wasn't there.

'Oi, Caldecott, just a minute—where the bloody hell do you think you're going?'

Eddie kept on walking.

'I'm speaking to you—yes you, you great…waste of space!'

Eddie was no longer sweating and had gone rather cold and dry. He stopped near the main gate where Mr Turnbull's sleek and gleaming BMW was parked. He looked at the car, glanced back momentarily at his father-in-law, then terminated his employment at Turnbull's of Bow in emphatic manner by putting a large dent in the rear, off side door panel with his right boot before disappearing into the back streets.

Chapter 11

Who Can I Count On?

'Only call on me as a last resort.'

Pterry's words sounded again and again in Eddie's mind as he marched resolutely through the hot, slumbering streets. Last resort? Eddie stopped for a moment to ponder his situation and was immediately filled with self-pity. He had no job, no friends and very little hair. His wife had become a stranger to him, his mother was dying, and he would almost certainly be facing 'assault and battery' charges in the morning. He set off again having decided that Pterry undoubtedly was his last resort.

So it was that, after a year and a half of separation, Eddie came to renew his long-standing love affair with the canal which had given him such solace in the past. If the canal had had eyes, she probably wouldn't have recognised her former suitor, who now stood on her towpath dressed in unfamiliar garb. A great deal of water had flowed under her bridges since Eddie had last trod her banks. Although she still moved slowly and sedately towards the Thames, like Eddie she herself hadn't escaped certain cosmetic adjustments to her outward appearance. These 'adjustments' became clear to Eddie as soon as he found that the hole in the rusting iron mesh fence at the end of Narrow Street had been replaced by a gate in a brand-new set of spiked iron railings, and that the mudslide on the other side had become a neat flight of steps with a hand rail. At the bottom of the steps, a municipal notice welcomed him to the 'Lea Valley Park.' A plump, pouting squirrel, the Park's logo, grinned slyly at Eddie from behind the acorn it was about to consume.

Nothing and nobody moved along the towpath. The strange grasses, bushes and flowers which used to grow there had all been burned back or poisoned, and their remains swept out of sight beneath concrete paving stones. However, a sharp eye would have noticed that cracks had already appeared in the concrete, and that pale, thin shoots had begun to push their way up towards the light. But Eddie saw only change, and it seemed to him to be irreversible. He hated the row of lifebelt holders ranged along the towpath like little red sentry boxes on sticks. He didn't even notice that most of the lifebelts were already missing, or that one holder had been snapped off at the base and was floating in the canal nearby. In truth, the adjustments to the towpath were inoffensive, but Eddie took them as a permanent and very personal insult.

'Terry,' he shouted, cupping his hands round his mouth, 'Mister T-e-r-r-y!'

There was no reply and still no movement except for the mercurial undulations of the water and the slow, silent progress of a jetliner across the sky.

Eddie set off in the direction of the chimney Pterry had led him to after his flight from Goliath and the skins, his sense of outrage against the perpetrators of change growing and fermenting in the afternoon heat. Nothing that he saw around him helped to diminish his rage. All the ancient, unconventional points of access to the towpath that he knew had been blocked by brick walls or iron railings, except for a few which had been smartened up and made official with steps and gates and notices. As well as the lifebelt holders and paving stones, uncomfortable-looking benches and accompanying litter bins had sprung up every few hundred yards. More disturbing still, gaps had appeared in the familiar skyline surrounding the canal. The declining sun showed them up like missing teeth—factory chimneys, warehouses, gas holders, cranes: all urban landmarks which were gone forever.

After a while Eddie passed the Beckford Dog Stadium to his left and entered the long, straight stretch which runs for almost half a mile up to the two great girder bridges which carry the railway and Carpenter's Lane across the Hackney Cut. Immediately beyond, at the confluence of the Cut and the Hertford Union, stood the old woodyard and its wharves, from which he would be able to see Pterry's chimney. By the time Eddie reached the bridges, his urge to see Pterry had become a craving, so that when he emerged from beneath their shadows to see that the wood yard had vanished, the shock made him stagger back a couple of paces.

The great black apron which overhung the canal, the ponderous mobile cranes which ran on rails to the water's edge, the massive warehouses which surrounded the yard: they were all gone.

The expanse of open sky which had been created couldn't have seemed emptier to him had it been recently occupied by the Great Pyramid of Giza because it meant that Pterry's chimney had also vanished. He began to run, slowly at first but building up speed like a charging knight. He ran faster and faster—faster even than when he had run to escape

Goliath and the skins through the graveyard. He was pushing all his pent-up frustration and disappointments into his pounding feet and lungs, as if by doing so he might outstrip time, turn the clock back and miraculously bring the woodyard and Pterry's chimney back into existence.

But Eddie wasn't able to learn the secret of time travel that day. When he reached the inevitable iron railings, which had been erected across the old entrance to the woodyard, he saw that not one brick of Pterry's home remained, and that a blanket of Rose Bay willow herb had already grown on the site like a bloody dressing on an open wound.

He stood before the railings, panting and sweating, bending forward, his hands on his knees, his frustration complete. Then he began to pace up and down like an animal, pausing now and then to stare through the bars with something of that expression of fierce wistfulness on his face that big cats wear in the zoo as they look out across hats, umbrellas and upturned, gawping faces. But lions and tigers can't use crow bars. New as it was, the fence had already been breached, and it wasn't long before Eddie was squeezing through a gap between two bent bars a little further along the towpath and plunging into the little jungle of willow herb. In his mind he was still nursing the hope that, although the chimney had been destroyed, there would still be some trace of its foundations with the help of which he might be able to locate the manhole through which he and Pterry had once emerged.

Then he saw it. A small, metal hut, almost obscured beneath the tall willow herb. He realised it must have been set up to cover the dangerous hole beneath Pterry's chimney which led directly to the Northern Outfall Sewer.

Eddie stood upright and craned his neck over the rosy fronds. Willow herb seed and down covered his bald, sweating pate, making it seem as if he had miraculously sprouted new hair. The sun was hovering not far above the flats on the Cranbrook Estate. Eddie cupped his hands around his mouth again and shouted in the direction of the hut.

'Mr Terry? It's Eddie here. Are you there?'

The words rebounded faintly from distant buildings as Eddie held his breath, straining to catch a reply from the metal hut above the thumping of his own heart. A waft of warm wind set the willow herb tinkling briefly, then all was silent again. Eddie let out his breath in a rush, gulped some air and called again.

'Mr T-E-R-R-R-RY? Are you there? I need to see you urgently!'

This time, as if in answer to his call, Eddie heard a sound behind him which had clearly been caused by something other than the wind. He turned slowly, half expecting to see Pterry standing there and eyeing him, perhaps tugging thoughtfully at his goitre. But although Pterry wasn't there, fronds of willow herb were still shaking to suggest that he might have been just a moment earlier. Whatever had made the sound had evidently disappeared into a particularly thick and tall patch of willow herb about twenty yards away, and just for a moment Eddie thought that he glimpsed that familiar elongated skull and its ruby eyes peering at him from amongst the hairy stems. He ran to the edge of the tall fronds, then paused for a moment as a primeval pang of fear ran through him. But he screwed up his courage and set off in pursuit.

The foliage was up to his chest right away, and in places

156

it reached over his head as he went deeper. Luckily the ground sloped gently upwards, so by standing on tip-toe or craning his neck every now and then, Eddie was able to keep plainly in view the shaking fronds which he hoped and prayed marked Pterry's progress through the willow herb. But after a few minutes' hectic pursuit it became obvious that he was never going to catch up with the rapid movements in the foliage. Panting heavily, he paused on a little rise from which he could clearly see how much Pterry had already gained on him. When he had caught his breath, he tried one last shout.

'Oi, Mr T! I know I look a little bit different, but it's me, Eddie. I just wanna talk to you. You said I could if I was ever in deep schtook—remember?'

To Eddie's relief, the movement among the willow herb stopped abruptly.

'Over here, Mr T,' shouted Eddie, leaping up and down and waving his arms. 'I'm here!'

For a few moments nothing happened, and Eddie thought Pterry might have disappeared down some concealed manhole, but then the rosy heads began to twitch violently, indicating that he was on the move again. However, this time the path led straight to where Eddie was standing. A smile of delight lit up his face, only to be displaced by an expression of bewilderment a few moments.

'Mr T?' he whispered, remembering Pterry's bandy, stunted legs and cumbersome wings—and wondering for the first time if such a body could carry its owner through the willow herb with the speed of whatever it was that was bearing down on him. Then, instead of Pterry, he saw the horned head and yellow reptilian eyes of Towser the

Triceratops. He turned to run, but it was too late. Towser's head caught him squarely in the backside and sent him flying through the air.

'Shiioooooooowwwwwwww!'

Eddie lay face down in the willow herb for a while as Towser sniffed, poked and prodded him. Then, content that his tormentor had been thoroughly vanquished and didn't pose a threat to his master, Towser sauntered off in search of tasty morsels in the little forest.

When Eddie finally staggered to his feet, the willow herb fluff had grown even thicker on his crown. The sun was balanced precariously on top of the two tallest blocks of flats on the Cranbrook Estate, and by the time it had slipped down the gap between them, Eddie had made his way to the westernmost extremity of the Northern Outfall Sewer. Although his backside was aching from his encounter with the little Triceratops, he was encouraged by the possibility that if Towser was acting as a guard dog, his master couldn't be far away.

He came across another new municipal notice on which the same squirrel with the pout and the 'come hither' eyes stared at Eddie. It read: 'Northern Outfall Sewer Embankment. Landscaped Footpath Planting Scheme—Stage 1.' Eddie looked around. He was already half way up the side of the embankment and close to the metal hut, which he now returned to.

The notice on the outside of the hut read 'Danger. High Voltage. Keep Out.' After Eddie had bruised both shoulders against its handle-less doors his frustration began to return. The last thing he wanted was another confrontation with Towser.

Three times he circled the hut, but the windows were high and too small for him to climb through, even if he could have reached them to break them. Exhausted, he leaned back against the warm metal, closed his eyes and let himself slide down into a crouching position. He suddenly felt very weak, and for the first time since he had left his desk at Turnbull's of Bow, he had no idea what to do next. Somehow, he had convinced himself that he would only have to return to the canal to find Pterry and then all his problems would be solved.

It hadn't worked out that way and now he was beginning to feel that he had used up all his options.

'Sorry, Reen love,' he said out loud, 'will you ever forgive me?'

The evening was so still that if it had been threatening rain you could probably have heard an umbrella opening in nearby Roach Road, but as the sky was cloudless there was no likelihood of this being put to the test. In normal circumstances, the chances of hearing an umbrella opening in the hut behind Eddie would have been at least a million times more remote, but that's exactly what he did hear—or thought he heard—and the sound filled him with renewed hope and energy.

'Mr Terry!' he shouted, sliding back up the wall. 'Is that you?'

No answer, not even the opening of an umbrella. Eddie stood up to face the handle-less doors and pounded on them with his fists.

'Mr T, I know you're in there. Open the doors for fuck's sake—I need to talk to yer.'

Still no answer. Eddie turned away from the doors and

159

looked wildly about him. The first thing he set eyes on was the new municipal notice which had welcomed him to the 'Landscaped Footpath.' He ran down the embankment at such speed that he had to hang on to the pole of the notice to stop him somersaulting over the fence into Roach Road. He spun round a couple of times before coming to rest face to face with the squirrel, whose smile remained fixed, despite Eddie's antics. It still didn't alter when Eddie began to push and pull the pole with almost superhuman strength, as if he had just consumed a can of Popeye's spinach. Eddie's face was also set, but with an expression of dogged determination, his eyes shut tight as he concentrated all his new-found strength into his arms. Down Roach Road windows began to open.

'Oi! Jackie Pallo! Give it one for me, will ya?'

A mother fetched her toddlers in from the pavement.

'Nah, it's Mick McManus!'

An indignant sleepy tom cat was whisked off its warm window ledge.

'Bleedin' vandal, you ought to be ashamed!'

One conscientious citizen ran downstairs and bolted her front door before dialling 999, but Eddie was oblivious to all this. He didn't hear the cheer which went up from the crowd of children gathered in the street when at last he wrenched the municipal notice from the ground. He didn't even see the two Smooves who were watching from a safe distance along the Outfall as he staggered back up the embankment with his prize.

For their part, the Smooves didn't recognise the man who had fascinated them once before in the bar of The Bloody Mary, but they watched with similar fascination as he turned at the top of the embankment, gripped the municipal notice like a lance in his right hand, then charged back down the slope at the hut with the handle-less doors.

*

Eddie was lying on his back looking up at the ceiling, where the last rays of the sun passed through the high, narrow windows to illuminate the clouds of dust raised by his sudden, spectacular entry. The point of his lance had passed through the doors and bounced off the opposite wall, loosening his fillings and sending him sprawling on the floor, which was already deep in shadow. Apart from him and the municipal notice, the hut was empty, but there was a sweet and sickly scent in the air, the unmistakeable whiff of freshly opened baked beans.

'Mr T?'

Eddie rocked forward onto his hands and knees. Then, with his nose almost touching the floor like a pig hunting for truffles, he set off in search of the black hole through which he and Pterry had once emerged from the Outfall. But after ten minutes scrabbling in the dust which covered the smooth, concrete floor, he had found no trace of the hole, nor even the slightest evidence of the tightest fitting trap door.

'Please, Mr Terry,' whispered Eddie, 'where are yer? You must be here somewhere.' There was desperation in his voice as he shaded his eyes and looked up hopefully, hoping to see Pterry hanging upside down, like a bat. But the ceiling was as smooth and empty as the floor.

At first Eddie didn't register the distant sound of the police siren. However, it grew louder and more persistent until at last, like the dreamer starting from his bed, he awoke to the reality of what was going on outside the four walls of the hut. He ran to the doors, pushed them open a crack, and saw two policemen scrambling down the embankment above him.

'For Chrissake, Mr T, it's the Bill,' squawked Eddie, slamming the doors shut. He turned to look around the hut, but it looked emptier than ever, and now that the sunlight wasn't coming through the narrow, high windows, you couldn't even see the dust moving. A moment later, the silence was shattered by the voice of the law demanding Eddie's immediate surrender.

'Come on, sunshine, we know you're in there, so be a good gentleman and open these doors before we 'ave to knock 'em down.'

Eddie put his back to the doors and spread-eagled himself like a character in a silent movie. Two or three hefty kicks from the P.C.s swiftly dislodged him from that position, sending him staggering forward to trip over the municipal notice.

'One, two, three and...' The doors bulged as the officers pressed home their attack. 'One more ought to do it, Sarge.' Eddie picked up the municipal notice, 'One, two, three...' and slid it diagonally through the push bars on the inside of the doors, effectively bolting them together, 'Ow! Sod and bugger it' came the voice of the law from outside the hut.

'All right sunshine, we can wait—but the longer we wait out here, the worse it'll be for you.'

'I'm so sorry, Reen,' said Eddie as he heard another police siren followed shortly by more size twelve boots arriving outside. Exhausted, he leaned against the municipal notice, nose to nose with the squirrel which now seemed to be grinning wryly, as if to say, 'Looks like the last laugh's on you, squire.'

'It just ain't fair, Mr Terry,' sobbed Eddie, beside himself with self-pity once again, 'I was in the shit up to me armpits, now I'm in it up to me chin. How much further do you want me to sink?'

'Up to your eyebrows, if necessary, Eddie, my boy,' came the measured reply, and at the same moment, the hut was filled with the scent of a thousand freshly opened cans of baked beans and the sound of the wind playing over the necks of a host of empty beer bottles.

'Mr Terry!' shouted Eddie, spinning round at the sound of that plummy, slightly pompous voice. There were now two deeper shades among the shadows in the hut—a jet-black disc in the middle of the floor and a ragged shape against the far wall. Two ruby coals lit up in the top part of the ragged shape as if an electric appliance had been switched on, though Pterry's eyes were glowing with a far deeper lustre than any ignition light that Eddie had ever seen.

'Am I glad to see you, guv'nor,' blurted Eddie in relief. And then, in sudden indignation: 'Oi, what's the idea of leading me on this... on this wild goose chase?'

Pterry raised an eyebrow in the dark.

'Sposin' you hadn't turned up...'

Eddie was abruptly cut short by the sound of a mighty blow to the doors of the hut which reverberated around the four walls and sent him tottering forward a few paces.

The forces of law and order had equipped themselves with a battering ram to gain entry to Eddie's castle.

'Come come, Eddie, this is hardly the time to be arguing

the toss. A couple more, good, solid blows and those fellows will be inside—good God, what have you done to yourself?' chuckled Pterry coming closer and inspecting Eddie's new clothes, specs, haircut and face fungus.

'That's my business, but...'

'No buts, just listen very carefully to me,' said Pterry firmly.

'No, you listen to me, Mr Terry. I...'

Another thunderous blow drowned Eddie's words and made him take another involuntary step forward.

'Don't move, Eddie!' Pterry's voice carried such authority that Eddie froze, one foot in mid-air. 'Now bring your right foot back very slowly—I don't want you going in there until you've heard my instructions.

Eddie obeyed mechanically, then looked down. He was standing on the very edge of the black disc, only now it was no longer a two-dimensional thing but had become a dark, echoing well which exhaled a warm, indescribably awful smell. Far down in the depths of it, little tongues of will o' the wisp flitted to and fro like fireflies. There was also an element so strange and powerful that it conjured an image of something dark and slick and shining moving inexorably forward like a titanic, endless worm gliding through infinite ooze.

Eddie swayed forward, mesmerised for a moment, then leapt back with a shout of fear and sat down to anchor himself more securely to the ground.

'Now then, Eddie, listen to me and listen well,' said Pterry, his voice calm but urgent and insistent, 'there's no room to take off in here so I'm not going to be able to carry you as I did before,' he continued, rubbing his goitre with a bony digit at the memory, 'besides, I'm not getting any younger and I think you've put on a stone or two if I'm not mistaken.' He looked pointedly at Eddie's paunch. 'So, you're going to have to jump.'

'Jump?' squawked Eddie, still breathing heavily with fright. 'Jump? In there?'

'Nothing else for it, I'm afraid, my boy. I'll go first and you follow. Take a deep breath and hold your nose. When you hit the Outfall, don't panic. You'll go in deep, but don't try struggling to the surface, just let yourself float naturally. Don't worry, I'll be there to grab you when you bob up. Piece of cake really.'

'You must be bleedin' jokin' Mr Terror. Jump in that hole? Shippam's Paste, I'd rathe...'

But once again Eddie's protestations were cut short by a blow, which almost burst the doors and shattered two panes in the windows.

'You'd rather WHAT exactly, Eddie? Fall into the loving arms of the boys in blue? I've been keeping an eye on your antics, and I know you're in enough trouble as it is. But I can't help you if you stay in this hut. Come on, old chap, "Per ardua ad astra" and all that.'

'Mr P-Terry, wait!'

'You are so tiresome, Eddie—PLEASE don't pronounce the P dear boy,' came the reply, then Pterry was gone, and Eddie was alone again. He crawled on hands and knees to the edge of the black hole and peered timidly into the abyss.

'P-Terr... sorry, no P 'ain't it? You there Mr Terry?'

Only the faint echo of his own words made reply. He struggled unsteadily to his feet, never taking his eyes off the flitting will o' the wisp which had begun to mesmerise him

165

once again. Nausea welled up in his stomach, filling his mouth with saliva and curling his bottom lip. Supposing Pterry had never been there. What if he had imagined the whole thing? Drool trickled from the corner of his mouth. But as if to reassure him the will o' the wisp momentarily looked like the golden heads of daffodils fluttering in the wind, and amongst them Maureen's face appeared, just as it had when he looked up from the grave on the first morning they met.

'Right lads, one more should do it. Ready now, on the count of three.'

The voice outside the hut seemed to Eddie to have come from miles away, like a long-distance telephone call—or perhaps even from another time, like a pre-recorded message or the speaking clock...

'One, two, three and...'

*

Maureen put the phone down, lay back on her bed and laughed until it induced such a fit of coughing that she had to flee to the kitchen to gulp water before laughing again. Then she clapped her hands over her head and jumped up and down as if the Hammers had stuck the ball in the net right in front of her. She gulped another glass of water down, whisked little John from his cot, cuddled him, raised him above her head like the F.A. Cup, cuddled him again and repeated the process until his wide-eyed amazement turned into a smile, then a gurgling laugh. Then she subsided into a chair with John in her lap and let another wave of laughter wash her helplessly away. There was a trace of hysteria in her laugh, but the mirth she was expressing was entirely real for the first time in many months—it wasn't the thin, hollow laughter which hides a heart full of pain and often collapses into tears. Besides, she had a right to be a little hysterical— her step-father's outraged description of Eddie's resignation was very, very funny. But her elation was inspired more than anything else by a profound sense of relief.

She had been deeply resentful of the conspiracy between Eddie and Mr Turnbull which brought them to Willow Close without her consent. Apart from the daily whispered comments and knowing looks which the neighbours indulged in, every time they saw her with the twins, or with John in the pram, she was horrified by the thought that the monthly mortgage repayment was dependent on the salary which her step-father paid Eddie, a salary which was little more than a bribe to make sure that Eddie remained respectable in his eyes.

She wouldn't have minded quite so much if Mr Turnbull had shown some real interest in fostering Eddie's career, but it soon became obvious that he was quite content to moor his son-in-law up a backwater and leave him there with the result that, after a few weeks at work, Eddie became bored and switched off completely. At home he hardly went out, particularly not to the pub, claiming that he was thereby doing his duty as a husband. Instead, he sat in the front room, drank too much beer and whisky and became grumpy. He knew he had made a mistake—many mistakes—but he wouldn't admit it. He had committed himself to a course of action, and he went on defending it in a tone of injured self-righteousness.

'I did it all for you, Reen—look what I get in return,' he

would whinge, whenever Maureen got fed up with him moping about his job.

'Why don'tcha pack it in then for Chrissake—we'll all move back to the Mansions tomorrow!' Maureen would answer, as often as not puffing on a fag.

'Chance'd be a fine thing!' chorused the twins, whose footballs were no longer returned when they flew into neighbours' gardens.

'Oh yeah? Do you suppose the bleedin' council would take us back now? Anyway, what about the baby?' was Eddie's invariable reply and escape clause, though he knew full well that the house in Willow Close was registered in Mr Turnbull's name. But the idea of coming face to face with Spider or anyone from the Samson was as strong a deterrent to moving back to Beckford as any other factor.

When Ethel Caldecott's cancer had been diagnosed Eddie had become bitter and resentful of everyone, even his father, glaring at them as if to say, 'why should you be well and my mother dying?' He had reserved his deepest scorn for Mr Turnbull, dismissing his father-in-law's offers of sympathy and loathing the extravagant bouquets of flowers with which he surrounded Ethel's hospital bed. When Mr Turnbull had offered to give him Willow Close outright, he had flatly refused, then immediately regretted his decision. But he was too proud to change his mind. 'I'll soon be able to pay the mortgage m'self, thank you,' he had bragged, knowing it was a lie.

Maureen had endured her pregnancy in this climate of suppressed malevolence and hostility. On the night when John was born, Ethel Caldecott's condition suddenly deteriorated to the point where it was feared she would die within a few days. The birth was long and painful, and when little John finally did arrive into the world, a month early, he had to spend the first few weeks of his life in an incubator. Under these circumstances—or even under normal circumstances – it would have been quite natural if Maureen hadn't experienced those tender feelings towards her child which every mother hopes for and expects. But nobody had told Maureen about the extreme forms which post-natal depression can take, so for the first few months she had mothered John mechanically, loathing the child and its endless wailing almost every day, and loathing herself even more for emotionally rejecting her own son. All the while, she had felt too ashamed to tell anyone what she was going through, least of all Eddie.

One night she had dreamed that she awoke to the familiar sound of John crying. She had lain awake for what seemed like hours, her anger and loathing growing with each passing moment. Then, when she had been unable to stand it no longer, she had got out of bed without disturbing Eddie, who was wreathed in whisky fumes, and crept downstairs in the darkness, feeling her way to the cupboard in which Eddie kept a cardboard box full of his DIY stuff. The bright red handle of a Stanley knife had glowed dully amongst the other shadowy tools,

She had seized it eagerly, then felt her way back upstairs to the bedroom. John had been lying in his cot, glowing with a strange luminescence among the dark bedclothes, bawling up at her, his contorted face framed by pudgy, clenched fists which he had seemed to be shaking at her in his rage. Using the very tip of the blade, Maureen had drawn a thin smile across John's throat, from one little ear to the other, and almost with the same movement she had taken the knife to her own neck. Immediately a dark halo had spread across the bedclothes framing the tiny white face. Although John could no longer make a sound, his mouth remained open in the act of screaming as his mother's blood fell like hot tears on his cheeks.

Maureen had awoken with the vision of that sad, pale little moon-face before her eyes. She had screamed herself, leapt out of bed and ran to the cot. John had woken up and began to cry as normal, but for the first time in his life, his mother hadn't resented him for doing so—instead, she had taken him in her arms and hugged him with real love and affection.

Eddie had slept soundly throughout the whole episode, though even he had noticed a sea change in Maureen when he finally awoke.

Maureen had known that she loved John from that moment on, though feelings of guilt and shame had lingered. But her new-found affection for her third son did not improve her relationship with Eddie, who became more irascible and distant than ever, almost seeming at times to be jealous of the attention which Maureen had begun to lavish on John. She knew exactly why Eddie had become so bitter since their marriage, but she also knew from long experience that he had to work it out for himself—and that he would absolutely refuse assistance from anybody else.

She had sometimes thought of going to see Spider and explaining the situation to him, but then she thought how enraged and embarrassed Eddie would be if he found out, and she realised this wasn't the solution. Eddie's wounded pride might even prevent him from resolving his problems.

Although she hadn't seen Spider or any of the others from the Samson since the wedding, she couldn't believe that they didn't have a good idea of what had happened. Gossip travels fast, and it wasn't as if she and Eddie had moved to the other side of the world.

*

Several hours after she had received the call from her father, the phone rang again.

'Hello. Do I have the pleasure of speaking to Mrs Edward Caldecott?'

'You what?' replied Maureen, taken aback by the old fashioned, aristocratic, slightly supercilious voice on the other end of the line, a voice which shouldn't have been familiar to her but which, in some strange way, she felt she had known for many years.

'I know this is going to sound a trifle queer, but...' the voice paused, in apparent uncertainty about what to say next, 'you don't know me, but I...well, I know you... after a fashion.'

'Whaaat? What're you on about for Chrissake?'

'Let me get to the point. Now there's no cause for alarm, but I have to tell you that your husband, Eddie, will not be coming home tonight.'

'That doesn't surprise me. Where is he?'

'I'm afraid I can't tell you that. You'll just have to trust me that he's perfectly safe and well, just a little, um... indisposed at the moment.'

'He's pissed, isn't he?'

'No, quite the reverse actually. Look, I'm most terribly

171

sorry, but I really have to go now. There's just one thing I would ask you to do if I may. Next Saturday evening, there's a programme called *Stargazers* on the BBC at six thirty p.m. Please watch it... and trust me, all will be well.'

'Oi, wait a minute...' Maureen protested, but the anonymous caller had gone. She shrugged, put the phone back on the hook and reached for the Radio Times. She couldn't say why, but that phone call had made her almost as happy as the earlier one from her father.

*

Later that night, a shadow passed silently across the full moon above slumbering Beckford, then swooped to set the clothes pegs dancing on the washing line in Willie the Wig's backyard.

Later still, Eddie slowly opened his eyes to find himself gazing down upon a fantastic cityscape, bathed in the light of that same full, yellow moon. Immediately below him, in the centre of a square formed by four low, windowless buildings, stood a stepped stone plinth. A thin metal pipe protruded from this edifice and breathed a languid flame which, caressed by the warm currents of the night, expanded and swayed like seaweed in some dim-lit underwater cavern. The walls of the four buildings were featureless except for a small door, no more than three-foot-high, set in the centre of each. Four narrow paths led from these doors and converged in the circle of light around the flaming pipe.

Looking beyond the limits of the square, Eddie could see the moon reflected in the slick surfaces of a dozen or so large, circular ponds.

Had the metal island in the centre of each pond supported cherubs or long-necked swans gargling jets of water, they might have passed for ornamental fountains in some city park. Instead, each island acted as the pivotal point for a long metal arm which passed over the water like a hand across the face of a giant clock.

Eddie could clearly distinguish the form of only two buildings beyond the ponds and the great square, though the jumble of shapes in the middle distance and on the skyline suggested that daylight would reveal many others. These two buildings were identical and dwarfed all around them, just as dramatically as The Mansions dwarfed the houses in Paragon Road. They were composed of only two features: a concrete ramp ascending in a semi-spiral to an immense folding door like a giant lift gate.

Thinking he was dreaming, Eddie closed his eyes and began to dream in earnest, though the scene inherited by his imagination didn't change. In fact, it seemed to Eddie that he had been watching for hours without anything changing but the shape of the flame and the great blobs of foam which the light wind occasionally skimmed from the surface of one of the ponds to send bouncing across the landscape. The longer Eddie watched, the more he became convinced that, at any moment, one or all of the doors would swing silently open, though who or what would emerge he could only imagine. But no doors opened. He dreamed that he closed his eyes and willed the doors open, but all that he managed to do was to wake himself up.

The scene below him hadn't changed materially, except that it was now broad daylight and the elements which composed it had lost the sense of portentous significance loaned to them by the light of the moon and the shadows cast by the flame. The great square was now no more than a rather tatty courtyard. The ponds were no longer filled with mercury but were grey and leaden. And the previously huge monoliths with their curving ramps now looked insignificant and puny against a backdrop of ornate chimneys, bulbous storage silos and smooth-flanked cooling towers.

Eddie closed his eyes again. He had caught a whiff of something which stirred recent, unpleasant memories, which started with a black hole and, for the moment at least, ended there. The air was rich with the stench of sewage, but there was another stink which ran through the main aroma like a thin blue vein across a particularly ripe Gorgonzola. It was the sweet, sickly scent of a freshly opened can of baked beans. This led Eddie's memory back from the brink of the black hole to the shadowy figure of Pterry standing in the gathering gloom of the little metal hut on the bank of the Northern Outfall Sewer. From there, his recollections ran like a film in reverse all the way back to Turnbull's of Bow. He groaned and put his hands to his face, disturbing from his nose not the aviator specs but his old Eddie Cochran shades. He took the glasses off and stared at them blearily, rubbing his eyes with his free hand. Having failed to remember why he should think it odd to be wearing them, he slid the shades slowly back into place.

'Ah, Eddie, my boy! Welcome once more to the land of the living.'

At the sound of that familiar, plummy voice, Eddie sat upright with a grunt of disorientation, aware for the first time that he really was awake. Pterry was perched on a trapeze which hung a few feet above the floor of a room that was at once very strange, and yet similar to one which Eddie had seen before.

'Am I dead or wot?' croaked Eddie, getting slowly to his feet.

'No Eddie, my boy, your time has STILL not yet come,' said Pterry laconically, 'though once again, not for want of trying!' he added ruefully, remembering his recent struggle to extricate Eddie's unconscious, sewage-soaked body from the Northern Outfall.

'Fuck me, are we back at your old gaff then Mr Terry?'

'Don't be alarmed, Eddie, you're not far from home—though a bit further away than before. This was once my second home, my country cottage, but alas it is now the only remaining example of Bazalgette's Patent Smoke Conducting and Filtering Chimney. It is situated almost exactly in the centre of the Beckford Sewage and Drainage Metropolis.'

'Another chimbly? Well, what's all that space age stuff out there then?' said Eddie, stooping and looking out of the window.

'Oh, just filter beds, pumping houses, a 'stink pipe' to burn off the methane—the usual sort of thing.'

Pterry was right. The Metropolis didn't look very space age any longer. It looked like home.

'Oh Jeezuz,' gasped Eddie, putting his hands to his head and remembering. 'Maureen—what about Reen? I've got to see her, Mr Terry.'

'Don't worry, Eddie—all in good time. She knows you're safe. Now then, we'd better start by getting you something to wear, hadn't we?'

Eddie reacted to Pterry's words like Adam to his first mouthful of apple. Realising he was stark naked, he coloured up and his hands rushed to cover his embarrassment.

'You might've bloomin' well told me,' he spluttered, groping for the blanket on which he had been sleeping.

'Oh come, come Eddie, don't be so bashful,' said Pterry.

'Yeah, it's all right for you though,' said Eddie manipulating the blanket into place, 'you've got your wings wrapped round you all the bleedin' time.'

'Oh, that's just for convenience's sake, dear boy—not out of modesty, I can assure you.' With that, Pterry unfurled his wings and reached up to a rope which hung down next to his trapeze, coincidentally revealing some particularly unpleasant prehistoric genitalia. A sharp tug sent Pterry flying across the room to the pile of cardboard boxes. 'You'll find everything you need in there, I think,' he said, taking a large, oblong box from the top of the pile and sliding it across the floor towards Eddie.

'No need to 'ave 'em gift wrapped chief!' chuckled Eddie, bending over and fumbling with the lid. A moment later, he leapt back from the box as if it had given him an electric shock. The blanket slipped from his waist, but instead of making himself decent again, Eddie just stood and gawped at the open box, the contents of which glowed among the surrounding tissue paper like sunken treasure fanned by diaphanous seaweed on the bed of some forgotten lagoon. The first to catch Eddie's eye was the yellow tweed drape flecked with black which Hooray Henry had given him in return for saving his skin at Pickett's Lock, but the box also contained a pair of recently pressed drainpipe trousers, a frilly shirt, a bootlace tie, a lamé waistcoat and a pair of crepe-soled shoes, silver buckles gleaming.

Eddie bent over the box again and, as if mesmerised,

reached out with a shaking hand to take hold of the tweed. 'B-U-D-G-E-R-I-G-A-R' he whispered, enunciating very slowly as he rubbed the cloth slowly, almost reverently, between finger and thumb to reassure himself that it was real. Then, as if a spell had been broken, he stood upright and pushed the box away from him. 'No! Whatcha tryin' to do to me Mr Terry? You know I can't wear this gear ever again— where'd you get it from anyway?' he shouted, the echo of his words bouncing to and fro from the walls of the chimney.

'Calm down, Eddie,' said Pterry, pulling on the rope beside him and hoisting the trapeze a few feet higher, 'they were at the cleaners the night your dear father-in-law came to the Mansions to dispose of your other clothes. Spider didn't know where you had gone, so he kept them.'

'Spider? D'ya know him?' asked Eddie, his voice softening a little.

'I know... of him, but he doesn't know... of me, so to speak,' said Pterry, tweaking his goitre thoughtfully.

How is the little bugger, then?'

'Quite a big noise down at the Samson, by all accounts,' said Pterry, sensing that Eddie was becoming more malleable. 'When you didn't come to collect them from his dry cleaners—and disappeared from his life altogether – he kept the, er, gear, thinking that it might come in useful to you one day if you ever returned.'

Eddie's face darkened again.

'Well, it won't. I'd be the laughing stock of the Samson if I ever wore them rags again. Come on, Mr Terry, just gimme the stuff I was wearing, will you, and you can dump this lot. I gotta see Reen.'

Pterry made an irritable clicking noise inside his beak.

'Now look here, Eddie, until very recently you and your clothes were bobbing along with the other turds in the Outfall. All the multitudinous seas incarnadine couldn't clean those clothes, let alone an ageing Pteranodon with a zinc bath and half a bar of Lifebuoy soap. It took me long enough to restore your body to its former glory. If you must know, I took the precaution of burning what was left of your clothes before they became a public health hazard, so unless you think you wouldn't be a laughing stock on the streets with what you haven't got on at the moment, I suggest you pipe down and get dressed.'

'Sod it!' Eddie became intensely aware of his nakedness again. 'Now, you look 'ere, Mr Terry,' he said sounding more aggrieved than angry, 'you promised me, that if I was ever in trouble, I could call on you. Well, here I am, and you haven't even heard of what sort of trouble I'm in before you start getting me into even more by givin' me those togs to wear.'

'Eddie, I know exactly what sort of trouble you're in,' said Pterry, in turn softening his tone, 'and believe me, putting on that jacket will be the first and most important step towards a solution. But let me tell you one thing. Neither I nor anybody else can help you until you stop feeling so damned sorry for yourself, so you need to sort that out first. Then—and only then—you may begin to see what other people have been going through as a result of what you pretend to yourself you've been doing on their behalf.'

'Eh?' said Eddie, scratching his head and looking understandably confused, but Pterry wasn't to be denied and proceeded to tell the tale of the last year and a bit from Maureen's point of view. Eddie listened without interrupting and, to his credit, felt deeply ashamed. When Pterry had finished, he sat down on the pile of cardboard boxes and leaned forward, his head in his hands. Between his legs, he once again read the words:

Crosse and Blackwell Baked Beans.

'Now then, remember the plan we were beginning to hatch in my...' Pterry's voice quavered slightly, '...in my other chimney, now sadly demolished? Eddie?'

'Oh, yes, sort of...' said Eddie, resurfacing from the tar pit of guilt into which Pterry's account of his selfishness had plunged him.

'As I said, we're going to have to face the world together, and it's time we started training for our big night. But first of all, you're going to have to acclimatise yourself to wearing these again, starting right now,' said Pterry, shoving the box of crepes and drapes in Eddie's direction. 'Oh, I almost forgot,' he continued, fumbling under his right wing, 'you're also going to need this.'

Onto the cardboard box fell a luxuriant, curiously coiffured head of hair.

*

Ted and Pterry are, of course, household names today. The virtuosity of their ventriloquist act, though its brilliance is undiminished, is now familiar to millions of TV viewers. Perhaps the memory of their first appearance has begun to fade a little in the minds of those who were lucky enough to see it, but there can be no doubt that their debut caused one of the biggest sensations that the world of showbiz has ever witnessed.

But there are some people alive today for whom the

memory of that night will never grow dim…

Down at The Bloody Mary, Dolly Skeat was in the middle of polishing straights when the duo appeared on the box, though it was little Henry who recognised Eddie first.

"Ere Doll, that's a familiar voice, ain't it?' he said, turning his face towards the flickering screen which sat in its eyrie above the door. Doll looked up from her work and promptly dropped the glass in her hands. It was the first one she had broken in ten years, but instead of tut-tutting and picking up the pieces, she just stared, open-mouthed, at the TV.

'I thought it was our Eddie,' said Henry, smiling enigmatically and reaching for the dustpan and brush, 'but 'who's the posh bloke he's talking' to?'

Dolly Skeat looked at Pterry and found it hard to answer her brother. Then she began to remember one foggy Saturday evening in November, a couple of years back, when Eddie had come into the pub looking as if he had just seen…

'A ghost,' said Dolly softly, thinking out loud.

'Oh,' said Henry, still smiling as he emptied the bits of broken glass into the bin under the sink.

He was thinking of Ethel Caldecott, who had made what the doctors feared might be her last trip to the TV lounge at the end of the ward in Whipps Cross hospital. Thinking that it might upset her, old Mr Caldecott hadn't told Ethel of Eddie's resignation from Turnbull's of Bow and subsequent disappearance although had she heard the news, she would have been overjoyed, like Maureen. As it was, she was sad and puzzled that Eddie hadn't been to visit her in the past few days. Her eyes had almost closed by the time Ted and Pterry appeared on the *Stargazers* stage, but at the first sight of them she sat bolt upright and grabbed old Mr C. by the arm.

'Harry! Look Harry, it's Ted!'

From that moment, the clusters of malignant cells which had taken a fatal grip on Ethel seemed to steadily relax their hold, beginning what the doctors would later describe as a miraculous recovery.

Harry had in fact fallen asleep, lulled by the shiny-suited crooner who had preceded Ted and Pterry.

'Bed? You ready for bed old gel?' he asked, waking up with a start.

'No Harry, TED. It's our Ted on the telly,' said Ethel pointing at the screen. 'That's my son up there,' she said proudly, turning her head and addressing the decrepit audience behind her.

'Which one?' shouted one old wag from the back, but it wasn't long before Ted and Pterry tickled them so much that the nurses had to be called to attend to various convulsions.

'Knocks spots off that Emu thing, don't it?' said the old lady sitting next to Ethel.

"Ere, Harry,' said Ethel, leaning towards her husband who was staring in disbelief at the screen, 'look at Ted's hair—it's all thick and lovely like it was when he was about twenty. Remember?'

'Oh, my bleedin' Gawd,' said old Mr C, not sure whether to laugh or cry, 'How could I forget, love…'

At the same time as Harry Caldecott was uttering those immortal words Spider Spinetti was taking an early evening drink in the sunshine of the deep-shadowed public bar of The Samson & Delilah.

'Oi Spider, 'ave a look at this will ya?'

By the way Spider jauntily stubbed out his fag and

swaggered round to the saloon bar in response, you could tell he had come of age as a Ted, though what he saw on the screen seriously ruffled his cool, causing him to drop his beer glass at more or less the same moment as Dolly Skeat dropped hers in another part of Beckford. He was thankful that the two moustachioed Smooves sitting in the corner were too preoccupied with the TV to witness his temporary loss of control.

'Wotcha reckon then? Is it 'im?' asked Stan the Man, handing Spider a cloth to mop up the beer he had spilled down the front of his drape.

'It's him all right,' whispered Spider in a high state of excitement. 'I knew Eddie'd be back. Didn't I tell you?' With that he did a quick toe and heel bop of triumph without the accompaniment of music.

'Yeah, but where did he come by all that hair, though?' rejoined Stan laconically, holding out a light to Spider who, fag in mouth, was now leaning back against the bar in an expansive pose, enjoying the show.

'I'll tell you where he got it,' said Willie the Wig who had joined them from the public bar, 'off me bleedin' clothes line, one night last week, without so much as a by your leave.' With that he whipped off his ratter to reveal a shiny bald pate. There was a moment's silence, then a peal of rather infantile laughter burst from the taller of the two Smooves. The sound died in his throat as Willie, Stan and Spider turned a collective withering gaze on him.

'Some'ing amusin' you, Sunshine?' said Spider, taking a menacing step or two towards the offending Smoove, who turned white and shook his head.

'In here you larf when I say and not before—geddit?'

The terrified Smoove nodded. Spider returned to the bar, looked up at the screen again and began to chuckle. His mirth spread rapidly to Willie and Stan so that soon all three were laughing uncontrollably. Even the Smooves, still pale and shaking from their brush with danger, managed a nervous grin when they thought the Teds were looking the other way…

*

Unlike others who, with a mixture of delight and incredulity, had seen Eddie on TV for the first time, Maureen just sat back and smiled, not registering a word of what he was saying, aware only that a crisis in their lives had passed. She hardly noticed that Pterry was there at all, though for all the other TV viewers the sight of him perched rather uncomfortably on Eddie's knee, a top hat balanced on his osseous comb and a monocle screwed into his left eye, created an irresistibly grotesque and unforgettable spectacle.

'Would you care for a lift home tonight, old boy?' said Pterry, for the first time unfurling and stretching one great wing and then another, drawing gasps of amazement from TV audiences up and down the land.

'Ta very much, guv'nor,' said Eddie jauntily, 'you can drop me off at the end of Paragon Road if you're flying that way—if it's still there of course!'

'Oh, don't tell me, dear heart, they're not going to knock that down as well, are they?' replied Pterry.

'Too right, I'm afraid, your lordship, most of Beckford will be dug up to make way for the link roads,' said Eddie with a sigh.

'Yes, and I'm afraid the Family Seat is not long for this world either,' croaked Pterry wiping a tear from the tip of his long beak, 'the last of Bazalgette's famous smoke conducting and filtering chimneys will be no more. But spare a thought also for poor old Leslie the Plesiosaur.'

'You mean Les the Ples, your lordship?'

'The very same—I've heard tell they are going to fill in his beloved Limehouse Basin to make way for a bankers' paradise!'

So, the story of the destruction of Beckford and the exploitation of its residents began to emerge before an audience of millions – and the phone lines to the national and international dailies began to hum with the news.

Chapter 12

Nervous Breakdown

The same heat which sat so heavily on the people of
Beckford that evening did no more than gently caress the
cheeks of the Rt. Hon. Sir Giles Jellicoe MP, bringing a slight
shine to his smoothly shaven skin and to his lightly pomaded
hair. From where he sat, tinkling glass in hand, he could look
out through the French windows across a swathe of lawn,
now dappled by long shadows, to a line of willow and elder,
which marked the course of a stream in whose shallow
waters fat trout hung almost motionless, white-lipped and
wide-eyed, awaiting Sir Giles's pleasure. Up above, in one of
the many bedrooms of his Hampshire manor house, Sir
Giles's three-year-old son Cecil lay asleep among a jumble of
expensive toys, his unruly nether regions still nightly secured
in a voluminous nappy. In the bedroom across the landing
from her charge, and equally secure in the handcuffs which
confined her to the four-poster bed, Cecil's young nanny
Amelia lay, as naked as the trout in the stream. She too
awaited Sir Giles's pleasure.

Normally an irascible man, domineering and not given to
attacks of bonhomie, two particular things had conspired to
put Sir Giles into something approaching a mellow mood.
First, he had recently defeated an application to extend the

nearby village of Dearden by building a small estate of terraced council houses. These humble, two-up, two-down red brick dwellings wouldn't have been erected in the meadows immediately below Sir Giles's Garden, or even in those beyond the stream, but would simply have constituted a small new detail in the top right-hand corner of the view from his French windows. However, Sir Giles had spent much of his life fighting to deny any other human being the right to appear in—and share his enjoyment of—the view from his house. He was therefore highly pleased at his success in ensuring that the feudal status quo would continue to be maintained.

Second, and even more pleasing to Sir Giles, was the confirmation of the compulsory purchase orders he had sought on large areas of Beckford, including The Bloody Mary and the whole of Paragon Road, the cemetery and The Samson & Delilah. Sir Giles had been involved in the plan to develop Beckford and adjoining boroughs from its inception – and in ironing out, with as much ruthlessness as was necessary, any little difficulties which arose, usually in the form of residents' or conservationists' protest groups. In fact, these 'difficulties' had proved far less troublesome than Sir Giles had any right to expect, given the enormity of the injustice which was being imposed on a section of London society—and the size of the remuneration which Sir Giles received from the construction company consortium for smoothing, quite literally, the path for their skyscrapers and yuppie flats. Opposition to the schemes had been fragmentary and uncoordinated. The plight of Beckford hadn't caught the public imagination, most people preferring to believe that East Enders' lives continued to be acted out as if in some

Dickensian time warp.

Sir Giles was about as likely to have watched *Stargazers* on TV as to have invited his gardener to join him for a gin and tonic, so he sat back in his chair, blissfully unaware of what several million people were watching at that moment, and of how their reaction to what they saw would affect his life. It was Lady Jellicoe's evening for late 'coaching' by the muscular young professional at the local tennis club: they had a tacit agreement whereby she wouldn't return to the manor house until the next morning. So, for the time being Sir Giles was faced with no more irksome a problem than deciding whether to lash the tranquil waters of his trout stream or the smooth expanse of Amelia's buttocks. The world was his oyster.

In the event, he postponed the process of decision-making by pouring himself another very large gin.

Sir Giles's dreams, especially when born out of the fumes of gin, often arose like demons to shatter the smug, self-satisfied exterior with which he presented himself to the world. That evening, as he lay in a stupor on the sofa, the demons chose to be even more mischievous than usual as his eyelids flickered momentarily shut.

It was a bright, clear day. Sir Giles was standing in a field of uncut grass, dark but brilliant green mixed with yellow. It was the water meadow below his house. He was on his way to do a little fishing, and although there was a strong wind blowing, all sounds were muted as if he had a heavy cold and was looking from his bedroom window at the riotous patterns which the wind made in the long grass. In front of him in the meadow stood the end-wall of a row of houses, a massive red brick expanse unbroken save for three small windows in the bottom, right-hand corner. It may only have been the end-wall of the humble terrace, the building of which he had succeeded in stopping, yet its uniform colour vibrating against the dark green grass gave it an awesome, monolithic quality.

Moving to his right, Sir Giles began to see the fronts of the houses. He walked towards them but saw no one. There seemed to be no street or pavement, their front doors leading straight out into the grass of the meadow. It was as though they had fallen from the sky.

When he got close enough to the first house to look in through a window, it seemed to him that the interior was derelict: a shabby staircase with varnish peeling off the banisters; furniture dry and cracked; white, opaque globes of dusty glass hanging from the ceiling, tattered net curtains at the windows. Yet the place had a serenity and calm about it, a warmth which was alien to Sir Giles's experience and which made him almost feel as if he would have liked to have lived there.

Leaning his rod against the wall, he tried to push open a door so that he could take a look inside, but it was stiff and seemed passively to resist his efforts. At last, he made a gap large enough to squeeze through. Inside he was in an alien, fragile world. The sharp, clear light of the day outside was filtered into a mellow silence by the dirt on the windows. Everything indicated that he was the first person to enter that room for many years, yet he had a strong feeling that someone—or something—was living there, perhaps sitting hunched on the landing up the stairs, or listening from the room beyond. Sudden fear entered his soul, and he quickly forced his way outside through the gap in the doorway which was threatening to close behind him.

Once outside, he found it hard to explain to himself what he feared. To his surprise, he felt concern as much on the behalf of whoever—or whatever—was living there as for himself. He didn't want it to follow him out into the meadow, not because it might have harmed him, but because it might have got lost outside. Sir Giles felt that it was looking at him from the house as he walked away across the meadow, so he waved at three empty oil drums which had been fly-tipped in a distant field, hoping that whatever was watching him would think that other people were on the way and would therefore be discouraged from coming out of the house. It seemed to work, and he walked on alone towards the stream, though not without a tinge of regret.

Sir Giles chose one of his favourite spots to fish, a bend in the course of the stream where the current had eaten into the opposite bank to form a deep pool. With a familiar thrill of expectation, he cast his fly, but before it alighted, he momentarily saw the far bank and the surface as the skirting board and the floor of the room from which he had fled.

Then the vision vanished, and he saw his fly fall gently onto the surface of the water. He waited for a few moments, then reeled in and prepared to cast again, but before he could do it, the room reappeared. Now he accepted that the room and the stream were interchangeable, and he thought perhaps there might be some trout hovering just below the surface in the far corner where the dust collected below the electric socket, so he flicked his rod tip and with some satisfaction saw his fly land in exactly that tempting spot. Then he was looking at the water again and ripples widening on the surface where a trout had risen for his fly.

He struck, and immediately felt the power of the fish through the arch of his bent rod. The urgent message flashed down the humming line which now disappeared between the gaps in the floorboards beneath the electric socket. The hooked fish forged up and down the room, threatening at any moment to break the line. Several times it passed below the skirting board on the far bank, and Sir Giles felt certain that his line would snag on the tangle of roots and electric cable just below the surface there. After a few minutes playing the fish, he managed to bring it close in below the chair on which he was standing, and he could see that it was a fine, big trout.

However, just before he was able to slide his landing net beneath its body, the fish gave a violent shake of its head and spat out the hook. It was free, but hung on the surface for a moment, perhaps exhausted from the struggle, perhaps unable to believe that it had thrown the hook.

Sir Giles saw his chance, and leapt from the chair at his quarry, frantically tearing up two of the dusty floorboards and reaching into the dark void below. He grabbed the great fish by its gills, jerked it out of the water and held it above his head like a trophy. He had won, but when he looked at his prize, it was no longer the sleek, shiny and mysterious fish with rainbow scales. Instead, it was a dry, dusty, squealing piglet. He felt sick to look at the fat, grotesque, goggling creature in his hands, throwing it back beneath the floorboards with a shout of horror.

Turning away from the stream, his feelings of revulsion were suddenly transformed by the beauty of the evening. The sun had set, and the wind had died away to nothing. As he began to make his way back through the waist-high grass, he saw little luminous things glowing where the shadows were darkest around his feet as if he was wading through the shallows of some phosphorescent sea. The violet air was intoxicating to breathe.

It had become so still that when Sir Giles first noticed the sound of the approaching *tsunami*, he thought it was only the blood in his head or the breath in his throat, but it rapidly grew into a roar which shook the earth. Then there was the wave, bursting through the treetops down the valley to his right.

It swept on towards the manor house, and he could only stand helplessly and watch as it hit the tall garden wall, sending up a huge sheet of water which seemed to hang for a moment before curling over and crashing onto the house beyond. Now he was running through the meadow, which was awash with the receding waters of the wave. The long grass and the boggy ground dragged at his feet and legs, making his progress painfully slow.

He was almost exhausted by the time he reached the house and had to stop for a moment to draw breath in the pillared porch. It was then that he heard that ominous rumbling sound again. There was another wave coming up the valley.

In recent years Sir Giles had preferred the company of trout to that of his family, but now his wife and son seemed the most important treasures in the world to him. He threw open the front door, shouting for Lady Jellicoe and Cecil to run for their lives. There was no reply. He ran from room to room, but there was no sign of them, and all the while, the sound of the great wave swelled, shaking the whole structure of the house. Water from the first wave sluiced around the floor, making an ornamental waterfall of the grand staircase and pouring down into the cellar. The cellar! It was the only place he hadn't searched.

Cecil, Lady Jellicoe and Amelia lay peacefully in hammocks strung between Sir Giles's wine racks. They must have been sleeping there when the first wave struck. It looked as if they were still asleep, but Sir Giles didn't even try to wake them – it was too late, he knew they were dead. The sound of the second wave was deafening. Sir Giles emerged from the cellar just in time to see it break on the walled garden sending an immense pall of water high into the air. It seemed to be curling slowly above the house, almost languidly, like those archive films of atomic mushroom clouds slowly unfurling.

*

'D-a-a-a-ad... Daaaad, Dadeeeee.'

Cecil's whining voice, a sound which Sir Giles wouldn't normally cross the road to hear, now seemed like a lifeline which had suddenly and unexpectedly been thrown to him as he was being sucked down into the deep whirlpool of his dream.

'Daaaaaaaaaad!'

Sir Giles grabbed at the sound and began to pull himself up towards the wobbling, mercurial surface of light above him. As he did so, he became increasingly and agonisingly aware of an intense hangover which, in the form of a red-hot G-clamp, had been attached to his spinal cord just below the nape of his neck. Each movement towards the surface seemed to precipitate another turn of the screw.

In the instant before he opened his eyes, Sir Giles would

have found it hard to conceive of a more gruesome situation than that from which he had just escaped in his dream. He was wrong. At first, as he was blinking in the early morning sunshine which poured in through the French windows, he could make out no more than the cherubic silhouette of Cecil's naked body against the light, standing at the end of the sofa on which Sir Giles lay sprawled, the remains of the gin still moistening his shirt front.

However, his eyes and nose informed him that Cecil's resemblance to a cherub ended with his silhouette, and that he was covered from head to foot in excrement. This discovery caused Sir Giles to start forward and fall off the sofa onto the shredded remains of Cecil's nappy. With an oath, he aimed a slap at Cecil's backside and immediately regretted doing so, not because of any liberal distaste for corporal punishment, but because the blow had transferred a considerable amount of excrement to the flat of his hand. A look of almost pious shock came over Cecil's face for an instant, then his bottom lip curled, his eyes puckered, and he began to wail.

'What in buggery do you think you're doing?' shouted Sir Giles, 'and where's Amelia?'

Cecil wailed more heartily.

'Amelia!' roared Sir Giles, staggering towards the door. The G-clamp had just become a gin-trap.

'N-n-nanny,' spluttered Cecil between sobs, 'nanny's on... on her bed. She... said she was...' Cecil's voice tailed away into a whimper.

'Whaat?' bawled Sir Giles. Cecil jumped and held up a pudgy fist, fearing another blow.

'She... she said she...'

'Well?' Sir Giles's hand was raised once more.

'She said she was playing... police... police something with you, Daddy.'

'Oh God,' said Sir Giles, putting his befouled hand to his head out of habit, 'Oh God.'

Trout or Amelia—he had just begun to remember the choice that had lain before him the previous evening.

'She...' whimpered Cecil, 'she's done poo poo, too.'

'Oh God.'

Sir Giles glanced at his watch, then ran upstairs to release Amelia.

'For God's sake, get yourself cleaned up—you can blame all the shit on Cecil. Here, take this.' Sir Giles left a crisp wad of notes on the bedside table as Amelia mechanically began the process which he had commanded. She had become used to this kind of degradation, which was invariably papered over with cash.

The crunch of gravel beneath the tyres of the Daimler belonging to the freshly 'coached' Lady J. was never music to Sir Giles's ears, but that morning it sounded like the bells of hell. He hastily stuffed his clothes into a bin bag, then dived into the shower just as she opened the bedroom door.

'It smells like shit in here darling—and all over the house!'

'Yes, it's Amelia's fault,' shouted Sir Giles from the shower, 'she let Cecil wander around without his nappy for a couple of hours. I wouldn't go upstairs for a while—it's not a pretty sight.'

'You're too soft on both of them, darling. Anyway, just a quick stop to pick up a few things before meeting Caroline and Char Char over at Stockbridge.'

Sir Giles offered up a prayer of thanks at this news. 'Have a fun time, angel.'

'Try to fumigate the place before I get back—and I'd give them both a good caning if I were you. Byeee!' she said, closing the bedroom door behind her. Sir Giles smiled grimly at this bit of advice as he wrapped himself in a dressing gown and swallowed a handful of aspirin, listening with intense relief as Lady J went downstairs.

Then the bedroom phone rang. Sir Giles thought twice about answering it, but in the end lifted the receiver and immediately wished he hadn't.

'That you, Jellicoe?'

The words were delivered in a thick southern drawl struggling successfully to escape from beneath a thin veneer of Upper East Side. At the sound of them, the gin trap around Sir Giles's neck immediately became a garrotte tightening rapidly across his forehead. The voice belonged to Jake Manderville of Manderville and Tonks, the construction firm deeply involved in developing Beckford. He was a man whom Sir Giles deeply despised, all the more so because he owed his own comfortable position in life almost entirely to the lucrative assistance he had given to Manderville, during the past fifteen years.

'Yes, this is SIR Giles Jellicoe,' he answered, emphasising his knightly status. 'Ring me later, will you?'

'Don't give me that SIR crap,' barked Manderville. 'You know you'd still be a shyster lawyer down the Old Kent Road if it wasn't for good old Uncle Jake, don't you? Uh? Uh? So, listen good!'

'Well, what in damnation do you want?'

'Want? Want? Have you read the papers this morning,

195

you dumb cluck? Obviously not or you wouldn't be so chipper. I suggest you read what they've printed pronto. I'll want an explanation in an hour.'

As 'chipper' was not a word which Sir Giles would immediately have chosen to describe his present condition, he longed only to get the hateful American off the line.

'All right, all right. Ring me in an hour when I've had a chance to sort things out here, will you?'

'RING you? Look Jellicoe, I'm at Heathrow now and I guess it won't take me much more than an hour to be knockin' on your front door. You'd better have got some ideas lined up by then, you get me?'

Manderville hung up just as Lady J slammed the front door behind her. Sir Giles listened from the landing at the top of the stairs, though he didn't stop to think it odd that, on a cloudless morning, she should be rapidly opening and closing her umbrella in the porch as if to shake the rain from its fabric. He had other things on his mind.

*

Sir Giles had been at pains to avoid any public meeting with Manderville, preferring to rendezvous privately at his country seat. So, for some years Pterry had been making regular, nocturnal flights to Hampshire in order to keep an eye on their machinations. He had found no difficulty in gaining access to Sir Giles's attic rooms via various chimneys, or in making a suitable spyhole for himself in the ceiling of Sir Giles's study.

By this means, Pterry had been able to predict the next batch of evictions and demolition in Beckford, and although

196

he could do nothing to prevent the destruction, he had at least had sufficient warning to move house before the bulldozers moved in. But now he was at a loss to know where to go if his last beloved Bazalgette chimney was condemned. So, it was with keen interest that he bent his ruby eye to the spyhole that morning, switched on his tape recorder, and began to listen to the conversation of the two men in the room below.

PTERRY TELLS ALL!

STARGAZERS DUO BLOW LID ON BILLION DOLLAR DEAL!

'What in blazes is this nonsense?' croaked Sir Giles.

'Nonsense? Yeah, well what about this?' growled Jake Manderville, slapping another tabloid onto Sir Giles's desk.

HE'S NO DUMMY!

PTEL THE TOFF FINGERS YANKS IN DOCKLANDS SCANDAL!

Up in the attic, Pterry's eye almost popped out of its socket as he tried to get a better view of the headlines and front-page photos of himself and Eddie. He had hoped for publicity, but now he was almost as flabbergasted by the extent of the coverage as the two conspirators below.

'Nonsense? It's the damned truth you great LUG!' shouted Manderville, pacing in and out of Pterry's circle of vision, while Sir Giles sullied his hands with the Mercury's newsprint.

'But... but... they can't prove anything from this,' spluttered Sir Giles. 'Not one chip of evidence... and nobody's named. They're just making it all up,' concluded Sir Giles with a thin, slightly hysterical laugh.

'No names for the moment, but you've not read the small print. If we don't finish the Beckford project before too long—and they continue to let the cat out of the bag—somebody may start believing them. And you know what that means, don't you SIR Giles?' barked Manderville, poking a finger into his henchman's queasy stomach.

'Oh, come now Manderville,' said Sir Giles, contemptuously swotting the picture of Ted and Pterry with the back of his hand, 'do you really think that anybody's going to believe this fat... Teddy Boy... or whatever he is, and his, his... stuffed stork?' Pterry's eyes blazed in the gloom of the attic, and he ground his long beak in indignation. 'Anyway, how on earth could they have got hold of any specific information? No one knows that you have been coming to meet me here, or what we've discussed. They've got to be bluffing. It's just a ploy to give their tuppenny-ha'penny show a bit more publicity. We've just got to sit tight for a few months, and it will all have blown over.'

'A few MONTHS! You think I can wait a few months?' roared Manderville, banging his fist down on Sir Giles's desk, making the paperclips leap into the air in fright. 'I've got guys outside my door in Dallas and New York who are not going to wait another few DAYS let alone months before they turn mean. These guys have a lot of big ones riding on this deal. You know what I'm talkin' about? A LOT OF BIG ONES! They want to know why we can't start building in Beckford right now—and I'm running out of answers. What d'ya think they'll say if I tell 'em we're keeping our heads down until some prehistoric dummy has stopped shootin' his beak off? I don't pay you a thousand bucks a day to hand me that crap. So gimme somethin' else and make it good!'

'You know very well why we haven't been able to start developing the sites in Beckford,' blustered Sir Giles, angry at seeing his trump card being wrenched from his hand instead of being played at a moment of his own choosing. 'But, as it happens, I have just obtained the compulsory purchase orders for the areas in question. Once the local residents have been evicted, there's nothing to stop us getting on with the job.'

'Nothing but that greaseball and his loud-mouthed, oversized rubber chicken,' growled Manderville.

Up in the attic Pterry attempted to control his fury by silently slicing off both of Jake Manderville's ears in his imagination. Unfortunately, in so doing his osseous comb knocked over a tottering pile of KNAVE magazines which Sir Giles occasionally consulted in his attic.

'What in hell's name is that?'

As he hastily put his eye to the spyhole again, Pterry saw Manderville stick his hand inside his jacket and pull out a big, black automatic pistol. Pterry rolled onto his side, expecting bullets, but instead heard Sir Giles's voice reassuring Manderville: 'It's only the squirrels. We've had them running around in the attic for years. Now for God's sake, put that bloody thing away.'

Pterry offered up a prayer of thanksgiving in memory of the dear departed squirrels who had provided him with a tasty supper on his first visit to Hampshire and now also with a good alibi for the occasional noise he made during his perambulations in Sir Giles's attic. He gingerly put his eye to the spyhole again.

Manderville was leaning forward across Sir Giles's desk. The big, black automatic lay in front of him. Rather than shouting he was now speaking so softly that Pterry could hardly catch his words, and he prayed that the tape recorder would pick them up.

'Listen good Jellicoe. The greaseball has to be

squeezed—until he croaks if that's what it takes. See if he has family, kids, wife. I have associates who can help you with this. Find them and find ways of putting the frighteners on them.'

'Isn't that a bit extreme?' quavered Sir Giles, loosening his tie and mopping his forehead. He could feel his throat swelling and beginning to close as his pulse quickened. 'I mean, surely, we can just buy him off?'

Manderville joined the tips of his fingers and made a roof over his gun. 'You give people money, they get greedy for more—I don't want the greaseball on the pay roll—capiche?'

'Now look, Manderville,' said Sir Giles, getting up and walking round his desk into Pterry's circle of vision, 'I don't want to be involved in any violence—certainly, none in which I can be implicated, at least. I... I have my career to think about.'

Jake Manderville's fingers collapsed onto his gun.

'You don't need to be implicated, you dumb cluck, at least not if you do things my way. As for your career, that belongs to me, not you. I decide if it develops—or stops right now.' His hands closed on the cold, black metal beneath them. 'Now, if you know what's good for you, I advise you to siddown and listen to me.'

Sir Giles pushed back a greasy skein of hair which had become dislodged from his immaculately slicked coiffure. He opened his mouth as if to reply, then thought better of it and slowly obeyed instructions, sitting back down in his chair.

'That's a good boy,' said Manderville, his fingers once more forming a roof over his gun. 'The greaseball has enemies,' hissed Manderville, lifting up one of the tabloids: 'With a face like that, he's gotta have enemies.'

Up in the attic, Pterry couldn't help himself grinning, despite the seriousness of the situation.

'All you gotta do is find out who they are and kinda... encourage them to take their revenge, so to speak. As it happens, I have some KKK boys with me who know a thing or two about encouraging people—and about taking revenge for that matter. I'll leave them at your disposal.'

Manderville stood up and tucked the automatic back inside his jacket.

'Oh, and one last thing—your idea about a museum of Beckford history—SCRAP IT! I don't want nobody knowing what the place was like before we came.'

'You can't be serious,' protested Sir Giles in a cracked, almost tearful voice, 'I've had staff working on the project for over four years. It's the best possible thing for public relations. We can't just...'

'I said SCRAP IT!' barked Manderville, reaching inside his jacket again.

'All right, all right,' muttered Sir Giles, utterly broken.

'Now I gotta get back to Dallas and tell my clients that everything's under control. Everything IS under control, isn't it SIR Giles?'

Pterry heard no reply, but Sir Giles must have nodded his agreement because Manderville continued in a low, gravelly voice, 'That's a good boy. The fellas'll be downstairs to make sure things stay that way. They'll be keeping you and Lady J. company for a while—I'm sure there's room for all in Jellicoe Hall?'

Manderville got up, closed the door quietly behind him and left Sir Giles alone in his study, crumpled dejectedly behind his desk.

Chapter 13

Come on Everybody!

A week passed, and day after day the sun beat down unrelentingly on the recently named 'Manderville Tower,' the vast, empty building which glowered over the Isle of Dogs. Its cooling systems weren't yet installed, so its concrete and steel structure was getting heated to temperatures never dreamed of by its creators. Every afternoon it seemed to exhale great breaths of hot air which took the dust and dirt of the city rushing up to meet the cooler currents above. By evening, Manderville Tower reached up into a thick, dirty yellow shroud which rumbled and flickered threateningly through the night before dissolving by dawn.

Late on Saturday night, a squad of 'workmen,' wearing Gas Board boiler suits and bright yellow hard hats to conceal their grapefruit skulls, began setting up road blocks to divert what little traffic there was from the streets surrounding The Samson & Delilah. In the early hours of Sunday morning, four transit vans and a large black BMW were waved through the barriers in Bladebone Lane and drove into Beckford High Street. The transits turned left and drew up quietly in Etty Street, a small cul-de-sac just across the road from the Samson. The BMW drove slowly past the pub, then did a U-turn and pulled into the kerb a hundred yards or so beyond the *Samson*, thus giving its occupants a clear view of both the pub and the transits in Etty Street. They could also look right down to the Isle of Dogs, where Manderville Tower was being silhouetted every few seconds by silent flashes of lightning.

The air was thick, hot and perfectly still. Unable to escape upwards, it was being slowly compressed by the ever-increasing weight of cloud above it. One of the filtration plants at the Becton Metropolis had been inoperative for several weeks, so that during this period, the heavy aroma of sewage had become an integral and inescapable part of the lives of the borough's inhabitants.

Beckforders are used to smells and had soon become acclimatised, but the aroma was particularly intense and pungent that night, flowing down into the deepest cellar, enveloping the tallest tower block and washing in and out of the mouths of sleeping Beckforders like sea water filling the lungs of the drowned. Only the four occupants of the BMW remained immune, existing as they did in their own little air-conditioned environment, as ignorant of the real Beckford as goldfish are of the family living room.

Nothing moved on Beckford High Street except for a few cats making for the fish heads which Mr Akrawi always left out for them in the back yard of the *Happy Sole*.

At 3.05 a.m., the street lights went out. The cats looked up, their pupils suddenly expanding in the unaccustomed darkness. A Tinkerbell spray of torchlight followed by six hulking shadows emerged from the back of one of the transits, slithered across the High Street, and disappeared over the wooden gates leading to the *Samson's* concrete beer garden.

The faces of the four men in the BMW glowed a dull and unearthly green. They were no longer goldfish in a bowl but aliens in a flying saucer, bent on extermination. For the first time that night, a deep reverberation of thunder became an audible accompaniment to the flashes of lightning which increased in frequency as the storm which had broken over the Isle of Dogs began to make its way up the Lea Valley towards Beckford.

Six more figures spilled out of the transit and followed the first group across the street and over the Samson's gates.

'Nuvver 'alf dozen comin' in the back way.'

Spider Spinetti, spotting from a first-floor window, passed on the message via walkie-talkie to those waiting in the stock room at the back of the Samson. The Teds there had already dealt with the first wave of invading skinheads with brutal efficiency, as though it was no more than a delivery of beer. Eddie and Delroy hit each successive invader over the head as they scrambled in through the open window, Willie and Dotun hog-tied and muzzled them, then rolled them down the barrel chute to the cellar and the safekeeping of Stan the Man. Now, they were pulling on the black balaclavas which the skins had been wearing.

The second wave were being despatched even more efficiently than their predecessors when the forces of nature dealt a cruel hand to the defenders of the *Samson*. Just as a third skinhead was reaching out to grab the hands of the balaclava-clad figures inside, a prolonged flash of lightning revealed that the proffered help came not from their companions but from men who wore velvet on their cuffs.

'They're waiting for us,' shouted the skinhead, dropping back amongst the others pressing behind him, 'get out of it!'

The four remaining attackers scrambled back over the gates and ran towards the transits, but before they were half way across the street, they were intercepted by one of the four men who had been waiting in the BMW. Something he said, combined with the persuasive power of whatever it was that he held to the head of the leading skin stopped their retreat.

A moment later, the two remaining transits disgorged their cargoes of skins, though unlike the first two waves these troops were armed with axes, baseball bats and sledgehammers. Four of them also carried a battering ram, in the form of a section of telegraph post, with which they proceeded to charge the front door of the *Samson*.

The High Street was instantly transformed by a bombardment of new light and sound.

'Light 'em up,' shouted Eddie to the Teds on the second floor of the Samson who hurled down a rain of lit fireworks—Sky Rockets, Air Bomb Repeaters, Star Shells and Mines of Serpents – which exploded with spectacular, if not deadly, effect amongst the wave of bewildered skinheads, enveloping them in a thick cloud of smoke and fire.

Then, as this first fusillade fell silent and the smokescreen began to clear, a vast African throwing knife of lightning blazed across the sky above the *Samson*, sending its multiple blades crackling to earth. At almost the same time, there was a high-pitched crack of violent, nearby thunder. Two petrol bombs burst against the walls of the *Samson*, and although the visual effect was more impressive than the material damage wrought, the sight of the flames emboldened the wavering skins and drew a great cry of triumph from those advancing behind them.

The skinheads, including the four with the battering ram, reached the front of the *Samson* and began to pound on the sturdy oak door as well as breaking any windows they could reach. A moment later, the first-floor windows opened almost in unison, and half a dozen Teds began flinging down heavy, brass-tipped darts onto the invitingly shaved heads of their adversaries.

'ONE HUNDRED AND EIGHTY!' roared the Teds as one unfortunate skin staggered away with three darts protruding from his skull. The skins faltered for a moment, but then the second wave returned wielding dustbin lids as protection. The double doors of the Samson began to bulge inwards, and although the darts were still taking their toll, the defences seemed to be on the verge of being breached.

'First floor, get your heads inside,' commanded Spider over the walkie-talkie, 'third floor, let 'em 'ave it!'

The third-floor windows swung open like the gun ports of a man-of-war, but instead of the snouts of cannon emerging, out came an assortment of sauce pans.

'One, two, three and...'

Down onto the heads of the skins fell the Teds' secret weapon—boiling Brylcreem and Tru-gel.

It was the twins' idea, and now Maureen watched them dancing with delight in the top floor flat of the *Samson*. The whole family had moved there for protection following Pterry's warning. A school history lesson was being enacted before their very eyes, the defence of a medieval castle brought bang up to date. The skins were in wild disarray—another deluge of boiling hair cream, fireworks and darts would have routed them, but just as fresh, brimming pans were being passed forwards to the windows, another brilliant flash of lightning ripped through the sky, accompanied by an almost simultaneous barrage of thunder.

In the same moment, Willie the Wig was thrown half way across the room, the pan flying from his hands and scalding the other Teds by the window. The lightning made the whole scene appear to be happening in stop motion. Amid the shouts and curses of his mates, Willie staggered to his feet. A dark stain was spreading across his pale blue drape just below the right shoulder.

Down on the first floor, Dick Beeson, the Tax Gatherer, lost part of his right ear as the window pane and frame splintered and dissolved in front of him. Then Delroy's face seemed to explode as his false teeth were ripped from his mouth in a shower of blood and shattered plastic. The bullet had passed clean through his cheeks.

'Get down for Chrissake,' screamed Spider, 'one of those bastards has got a bleedin' shooter.'

Another burst of gunfire which raked all floors of the Samson gave Spider's command even greater force. Now that the aerial bombardment had stopped, the skins redoubled their assault on the ground floor. Goliath, wielding a baseball bat wrapped with barbed wire, had managed to crawl in through a broken window and was in the process of unbolting the front door when he heard a familiar voice.

'Oi, grapefruit, shouldn't you be in bed with your muvver?'

Goliath turned to find Eddie nonchalantly leaning against the bar, illuminated by a flash of lightning like a pantomime villain. He had a billiard cue in one hand and the *Samson's* dartboard in the other. Goliath began to snort with pent up hatred, and his eyes blazed with excitement at the thought of taking revenge for the indignities that had been inflicted on him at the *Happy Sole* and in the cemetery.

'Come on then, sunshine! Ay, Toro toro!' taunted Eddie, stepping out into the middle of the saloon and slanting the billiard cue like a toreador's sword. Goliath's bovver boots rattled the floor boards as he charged Eddie across the shadowy bar, swinging his baseball bat above his head and bellowing with rage. At the very last moment, Eddie raised the dart board to take the blow from the descending barbed bat which became stuck fast in the board.

'Ay toro!'

Goliath paused for a moment to wrench his weapon free, giving Eddie just enough time to whack him on the backside with the billiard cue as he went past.

'Ay toro, toro.'

With a blood curdling oath of pain and rage Goliath turned, ready for another attack, but now Eddie had whipped off his drape jacket and was pacing back and forth, in full bull baiting mode, twirling his billiard cue above his head.

'Ay toro, toro, toro.'

Blinded with rage, pain and humiliation, what little sense Goliath possessed had long since flown out of the shattered window, so when he charged again, Eddie knew he had his man. As Goliath, running at full tilt, raised his bat to strike, Eddie threw his drape jacket in his face and at the same time shoved the billiard cue between the giant's legs, tripping him and sending him sprawling, not onto the floor of the bar, but through the trap door which Eddie had left open.

The sound of his bald skull connecting with the metal casks in the cellar provided Eddie with a frisson of satisfaction before he slammed the trap door shut and bolted it from above. At the same moment, the battering ram almost burst through the doors which Eddie had so heroically defended. He knew that if the skins got inside, it would all be up for the defenders.

However, three floors up, it was Spider Spinetti's turn to play the hero. Disobeying the order he had given just a moment before, he stood up, coolly strode over to the window to make sure the skins were immediately below, then went back to the stove where two large saucepans of hair cream were still bubbling away.

Manderville's sniper, peering through the night sight of his automatic rifle as he leaned over the roof of the BMW, spotted Spider almost immediately. He didn't fire straight away though, waiting until Spider returned to the open window, presenting the easiest of targets. He inhaled smoothly, held his breath for a moment and squeezed the trigger.

The umbrella which opened above the gangster, in the form of Pterry's great wings, didn't protect him from the big drops of rain which had begun to fall on Beckford. However, by ripping the rifle from his hands, Pterry did ensure that he would only be charged with attempted murder when he stood trial, together with all the others who attacked the *Samson* that night and who didn't manage to escape. It also saved the life of Spider Spinetti, allowing him to pour the contents of his saucepans onto the heads of his enemies who, with a great cry, dropped their battering ram and ran. But perhaps most important of all, Pterry was now carrying a vital piece of evidence up into the sky. The rifle, together with Pterry's tape recordings and other exhibits, would go on to ensure the conviction of Jake Manderville, Sir Giles Jellicoe and many of their associates.

Thus, Beckford was saved from the immediate destruction and appropriation it had been facing. The events that took place that night rapidly became known as the Battle of Beckford, and the names of the Teds who so valiantly defended The Samson & Delilah—and the honour of Beckford – will forever be enshrined in Beckfordian folklore.

*

Down on the Isle of Dogs, the storm drains had burst a few hours earlier and the flood waters had been burrowing away at the unprotected foundations of Manderville Tower. At about the same time as Pterry seized the hit-man's rifle, the great empty edifice of glass and concrete gave out a prolonged sigh and sank slowly, almost thankfully, into the Limehouse basin, like a weary old man lying down for the night.

Inevitably this disaster called into question the safety of the other high-rise buildings which had been proposed by Manderville Holdings. This, together with the trials of those responsible for the Battle of Beckford and the revelations which Ted and Pterry continued to make, helped to put the concept of a shiny new corporate Beckford on hold, for the time being at least.